FULL DRAW

DRAW

STEVE CHAPMAN

A special thanks to my daughter, Heidi Chapman, for her editing abilities.
Also, thank you to Annie Chapman, Nathan Chapman, Amy Carlson, Ilene Wilson, Susie and Zane Carson, Joe Goodman, David Brown, Don Scurlock, and Eddie Richey for their guidance in the details.

Front cover painting and design, back cover design, and internal illustrations by:
Ed French/Cotopaxi, Co.

Page design and set up: Ed Maksimowicz/Mak. Design / Nashville, TN.

Library of Congress Cataloging-in-Publication Data
Chapman, Steve 1950-
FULL DRAW/ by Steve Chapman
1. Nature 2. Hunting 3. Family 4. Fiction
ISBN 0-9653274-0-X

DEDICATION

This book is dedicated to the hunters who are willingly sacrificing their days in the field for the sake of caring and providing for those they love. Until another morning finds them in the hunter's woods, may the reading of these pages somehow serve, if only in a small way, to fill the gap. May God honor their faithfulness.

ABOUT THE AUTHOR

Steve Chapman, born in West Virginia and now residing near Nashville, Tennessee, has been an avid hunter for thirty five years. In his words, "A day in the woods is like a week's vacation! It's therapy for the soul!"

In 1975 he married a high school friend named Annie Williamson. Their shared interest in music began to blossom and today the two of them oversee S & A FAMILY, Inc., an organization formed to encourage families through music and lyrics. With over twenty recorded projects to their credit, they travel to nearly 100 cities annually, presenting their concert of songs and stories about family life.

Their home-schooled children, Nathan and Heidi, have graduated from high school and are presently spending their fall, winter, and spring seasons at a college four hours ("laundry distance" as the kids say) from home.

In 1997 Steve was invited to be on the pro-staff team of API Outdoors, Inc. of Tallulah, Louisiana, and he endorses their quality line of treestands and other hunting related products.

"Whether it's bow hunting the whitetail deer or trying to entice a gobbler in close with a box call, I hope I'm able to enjoy God's great outdoors for as many days as He'll give me!" Steve says.

CHAPTER ONE

Nearly twenty minutes had passed since the mature buck appeared down the ridge. The big woods were clear enough, even with the early October foliage, that Joe Tanner was able to spot the rack which the heavy whitetail sported. He had seen the huge animal a time or two during his scouting trips before archery season opened. The velvet was gone from the antlers, and the 10 points glistened in the morning sun. Joe was grateful for the encounter. His heart was about to explode with excitement as his left hand tightened on the grip of his compound bow.

The large number of white oak acorns that laid on the forest floor, like candy on a plate, caused the deer to slowly feed toward Joe's treestand. While the animal's appetite was being satisfied, Joe took the opportunity to begin rising to his feet, hoping that no creaks or snaps would result while shifting all of his weight onto the platform that towered eighteen feet above the ground. Finally, with the mission accomplished, he stood motionless as the deer intermittently fed, then raised his head to scan the woods for danger. The awesome creature did not suspect, in the least, that the keeper of his fate was looming above him, and he continued to feed toward the hunter's pounding heart.

Joe was relieved to see that the old buck was alone. There were no other sets of eyes to detect his movements...no other witnesses to their meeting. The rendezvous of life and death was to be a private matter, at least until Joe got back to his home in the city of Grandville and rejoined his wife, Evelyn, and their three teenagers. He forced himself not to rehearse the story of his hunt before it unfolded. He had made that mistake before.

Finally, the buck was close enough that Joe began hearing the light crunch in the crisp, dry leaves that a large four-footed animal makes as it walks through the woods. The sound sort of "faded up," as if controlled by the volume button on a TV remote. He considered it a nice change, for once, to not be surprised by the distinct noise. On many occasions, that tell-tale crunch had shocked him into a state of alertness, as serious as a dentist's probe pressing into a soft cavity. But whether it came gradually, or by surprise, it was hearing that sweet and exciting sound that caused Joe to want to return to the woods as often as he could.

At 35 yards out, and still approaching his position, the deer suddenly stopped. Something got its attention and Joe was concerned. He asked himself, "Which one of the deer's senses was alerted?" It didn't appear that the buck's hearing was aroused, because its ears weren't independently twisting like radar. "Did he see something?" Joe wondered. Moving only his eyes from side to side, he scanned the woods and saw nothing unusual in his field of view. "Maybe something is behind me," he thought.

Joe's joy returned when the deer seemed to relax, but it lasted only a moment. This time, the old buck revealed one of the reasons he had survived five or six deer seasons in the Giles County hillsides. He raised his nose to the sky and sniffed the air. He knew something was out of order. Joe's confidence in the procedure which he had used to eliminate his own revealing human scent was beginning to dwindle. He had showered with scentless soap, and had stored his camo clothes in tightly sealed bags of dried oak leaves for weeks before the season opened. His rubber boots were well seasoned. Still the buck seemed wary. "What did I forget?" he worriedly asked himself. Joe knew that the nose of an experienced deer could detect anything from the lingering smell of toothpaste to the faint aroma of oil drops clinging to a knife blade that's been

8

sharpened on a whetstone. Joe decided that he had done his homework as best he could. The old storehouse of intelligence that stood on four legs beneath him was simply trained by time, and other humans, to know something unusual was in his presence.

The sight of the big buck was reason enough for all of his senses to shut down, and refuse to cooperate. However, in that incredible moment, somewhere deep within, he was experiencing a strange calm. It wasn't a type of poise that settled the fleshly nerves, because he was still extremely excited, and had a wildly racing heart to prove it. Instead, it was a peace founded in some important characteristics of a mature hunter. First, he had practiced shooting his bow for hours in his backyard. He had destroyed a 3D target, and had totally unraveled a burlap bag of rags with hundreds of shots. He knew how to hit a mark. He was prepared in the art of picking a spot on the deer and concentrating on it. He was ready!

Secondly, he was aware that he had to overcome the temptation to look too long at the antlers. Past encounters with the thief of concentration, which Joe laughingly called "the rack attack," had taught him well. It was a fatal distraction, one which he knew would take some serious discipline to avoid. He had learned that in order to maintain steady emotions, he could not allow his eyes to wander away from the area behind the shoulder of the deer.

Thirdly, and most importantly, his calmness was rooted in an inward resolve that no matter what transpired in the minutes that followed, it had already been a great day in the woods! He was determined to simply enjoy his participation in a course of events that was bound to pass.

With his attitude correctly in place, Joe cautiously checked the arrow's position on the bow's rest. He glanced at the finger tab on his right hand to make sure it was properly placed on the string. Then once again, he mentally went through the steps to full draw. All that remained for the hunter was to wait patiently for the deer to turn its body broadside, and present him with a shot that would allow him to put its vitals in his peep sight.

The deer finally took a few steps. Whatever the scent might have been that caught his attention earlier, it was apparently not dangerous enough to make him run. Still, the buck's gait was slow and deliberate, the kind of movement a whitetail makes that informs the hunter that his window of opportunity is closing. The deer suddenly stopped, stood broadside about 25 yards away, and was looking straight toward the tree that held Joe's stand. He knew that to make any attempt to move when there was nothing between himself and a deer's eyes was a fruitless endeavor. In some cases, all it took was an odd shape, or an unfamiliar silhouette, to cause a deer to spook and run away. He had to trust that his dark brown and green face paint, and his camo clothes and hat, were doing their job in fooling the buck's skillful eyes.

What happened next fostered some very mixed feelings in Joe's heart. In all the years he had hunted, he had come to love a great number of things about the process. However, he discovered there were some elements of it that could be quite irritating. Such pretty, little, annoying creatures as chipmunks and squirrels that could detect his presence in the woods and tattle-tale on him had left him very frustrated at times. Then there were the hair-brained hunters who, without permission to be on the property, would wander under his stand, fully aware that they were trespassing, yet offering no apology. Add to that the pesky little gnats and mosquitoes that could make a decent man say things under his breath that required repentance. He had suffered many exits from the woods poked full of itching holes and feeling defeated by nature's tiny winged terror.

But that morning, one of the most dreaded destroyers of any good hunt made itself known. It was a dog. From the opposite hillside, behind the buck, about 400 yards away, came a series of healthy yelps. Joe whispered to himself, "Oh! No! The canine curse!"

However, the unexpected sound of the barking intruder turned out to be, at least in that case, the welcomed voice of "man's best friend." Joe was surprised to find himself basking in the glow of the disturbance when the noise made the deer bristle and turn its head to look in the dog's direction. With the buck's eyes looking away, Joe quickly and quietly lifted his compound bow out of the short holster that hung from his belt and came to full draw.

"Pick a spot" was all he allowed himself to think. As he looked through the tiny hole in his peep sight, he focused on the white 20 yard pin, and to allow for the extra distance that the arrow would have to travel, he placed it on a spot about 4 inches above the heart area of the big buck. Methodically, Joe let go of the string and the bow recoiled in his left hand. Within an instant, the neon green and yellow plastic fletching on the rear of the aluminum arrow disappeared in the deer's brownish fur. The woods exploded. Leaves and dirt flew up under the buck's hooves as he kicked high and wheeled around, then headed out of sight, back down the ridge from where he had come.

Fifteen to twenty seconds passed and silence fell once again in the woods. Joe longed to hear the crashing sound that a deer makes when it expires on a "dead run" and piles up onto the forest floor. However, nothing happened. There was only unsettling stillness. He was confident that his broadhead had done its deed, but he also knew that the buck was strong, smart, and scared enough to go as far as he could from where he had encountered the sudden harm.

Joe was surprised, at first, that the deer chose to run toward the dog. But then he reasoned, "Who, or what, would be thinking clearly if there was a sudden stinging in the lungs?" He assumed that the buck had somehow gathered its senses, taken the canine's presence into consideration, and somewhere, out of his sight, had made a turn. But to where it might have gone, he didn't know. His only hope was for a good blood trail.

CHAPTER TWO

As Joe passed through the first two minutes following the shot, a thousand thoughts went through his mind, but none of them took root. He just stood there swimming in emotions. It reminded him of the feeling that settles in on a person after they have successfully, but barely, avoided a serious car accident. They're calm at first. Then, about three miles down the highway, when reality returns, the awareness of what could have happened causes the legs to grow weak, the hands to shake, and the palms to drip with sweat. Feeling no less rattled in the excitement generated by the encounter with the big buck, all Joe could do was simply sit down on his treestand seat and attempt to recover a steady heartbeat. He was loving every minute of it!

After he replayed the shot over and over in his mind, and was sure that it was a good hit, Joe put his head back on the tree bark and took a deep breath. At the end of a lengthy sigh, he gritted his teeth, clinched his fist, and quietly screamed a particular word, one he had often heard his sixteen year old son say after sinking a long three point shot on the basketball court. "YES!" It felt so good, he said it again. "YES!!" Then he looked through the leaves above him into the brilliant blue October sky and whispered a prayer of deep gratitude. "Thank you, Lord!"

Joe's post shot procedure was tried and true. If he saw the deer go down, he waited only fifteen minutes before leaving his stand. If it went down and audibly "crashed" in the leaves, but out of the range of his eyes, he allowed 45 minutes to pass before finding the deer. If the animal disappeared completely out of sight, and no sound was heard that indicated it fell onto the forest floor, then he waited at least an hour. Knowing that the next sixty minutes would pass at a snail's pace, he forced himself to relax.

Joe checked the time and began his vigil. To pass the minutes, he decided to start with a snack. His 46 year old heart would not allow him the delicious luxury of a chocolate bar. One too many sweet celebrations in the past had yielded a stern warning or two from his doctor. His compliance to a better diet was made easier, however, when, during one visit, the doctor said, "If you wanna keep climbing into those trees and terrorizing Bambi's daddy, you better tend to your *ticker!*" That was all it took. Joe decided to change his dietary ways. As he sat in his physician's waiting room and reluctantly read the low fat rules he had to follow, he couldn't help but wonder if Evelyn may have put those words of warning in his doctor's mouth. He knew his wife loved him enough to pull that kind of trick. At any rate, for a snack, an apple had to do.

Then there was the matter of completing the big game tag attached to his license. He dug in his shirt pocket for his pen and started to fill it out, but decided to wait. He knew it wasn't wise to count his points before they were mounted. Instead, he decided to lower his bow to the ground and climb down out of the treestand. He attached his light brown lowering string to the end of his bow, but then he hesitated. He thought to himself, "What if that deer is only wounded, and disoriented enough to wander back by me? It's happened before! I better sit right here and wait!"

As he sat quietly and absorbed the sounds of the mid-morning woods, Joe's mind drifted from thought to thought for the forty five minutes that remained. His attention first went to Bob Gleason and how kind it was of the elderly gentleman to permit him to hunt on his 800 acres. The land had been in the Gleason Family for nearly a hundred years.

Joe's heart was saddened by the fact that Bob was a widower.

His wife, of nearly fifty years, took ill with a lung disease and died, leaving Bob alone in their big, two story, white house. He didn't allow the place to change much, inside or out, in order to serve his fond memories of the woman he cherished so greatly. His attention was especially directed at maintaining the flower garden that Sarah Gleason had so carefully created. It was his show of respect for her beauty, which he loved to remember.

The wood frame house was a handful to take care of, but Joe knew Mr. Gleason valued his chores, since they helped occupy his thoughts. Joe considered his assistance with odd-jobs around the farm, like mowing the fields and cutting firewood, as both emotional therapy and a grand opportunity to show good faith as a land user.

Joe looked at the trees that surrounded him and imagined, if they could have talked, what tales they might have told about the four Gleason kids who once played in the woods where he sat. He also wondered which of them might be the next to surprise Bob by showing up unannounced. His children were very good about coming in to see their dad, and keeping tabs on his bachelor-hood.

Then, for some reason, a man named Earl Potter came to Joe's mind. He was an unmarried man, somewhat aloof, and Joe had never been able to get to know him as well as he liked. Earl had moved into the area a little over four years earlier as a younger gentleman in his late thirties, and seemed to be a good neighbor to Bob. He was at the Gleason home when Sarah said farewell to her husband and children. Before she passed away, Sarah freely told everyone in earshot, including Earl, how that Jesus had gotten her "all cleaned up inside and ready for heaven," and that He wanted to do the same for everyone she knew. Earl politely endured her preaching, but to Joe's knowledge, he had never accepted the "gospel according to Sarah." Bob had expressed a time or two how grateful he was that Earl was nearby.

Joe's thoughts of Sarah continued. His memories of her were like priceless treasures in his heart. He had a bond with that old saint that could not be severed by her passing. He knew he would see her again someday, and smiled at the comforting thought that with her new body, Sarah could breathe deeply with no trouble. As his Sunday School teacher, she had instructed him in his impressionable years, and the seed of eternal hope in the Savior took root, and bore good fruit in Joe's late teens. He wondered if she somehow knew he was thinking about her as the time ticked by in his treestand. Only seventeen minutes remained in the wait.

Joe rummaged through his pockets to make sure he had his hot pink, plastic ribbon he used for tracking the blood trail he hoped he would find. As he did so, he had a few more interesting thoughts. One, if he found the deer, what would his two hunting buddies say when they saw it? He knew what L.D. Hill would do. He would drop to his knees and, as if bowing to a king, he would pay homage to the hunter. That was L.D.'s comical way of congratulating his comrades on their hunting success. He did it even if the deer was antlerless. His carpenter friend believed that any animal that was taken with a bow and arrow, and headed to the freezer, was a trophy. Joe liked L.D.'s attitude and shared it with him.

Then there was a southern gentleman, and bank manager, a transplant from the rolling hills of Georgia, named Bill Foster. Joe loved his "mountain manners" and he knew that when Bill saw the deer, he would just grunt and spit. Joe chuckled inside when he recalled the day they first met. It was in the halls of their old high school, and Bill was a new arrival. Joe looked at his 6'4" frame, peered up into his eyes, and jokingly said, "Would you do me a favor? Please... don't ever get mad at me!" Bill innocently assumed he was serious and answered with a gentle voice, and a drawn out southern accent, "All...right!"

Secondly, Joe's thoughts turned from jovial to somber as he

recalled what had happened the night before in his hometown of Grandville. Having a population of around twenty thousand, the peaceful little city wasn't used to the kind of violence it had experienced. Near closing time, two armed men entered Harper's Grocery and demanded the day's cash earnings. When a patron named Phillip Simpson attempted to squelch the robbery, the two thieves made their criminal intentions perfectly clear when one of them buried two rounds from a heavy caliber pistol into the would be hero. Needless to say, the assailants made off with a significant amount of cash. At news time on the regional TV station, it was reported that Mr. Simpson was in very critical condition at the county hospital, and his chances of survival were dangerously slim.

Joe didn't know the bystander, but he whispered a prayer for the man and his family. His thoughts about the whole matter were depressing, and it didn't help any to recall the report that the criminals had escaped. The unwelcome news was confirmed that morning as Joe passed through a police road block on his way to the Gleason Farm. Around 4:15 a.m., Trooper Lance Wilson greeted Joe at his driver's window. "How are you doing, Mr. Tanner? I guess you know why we're out here at this ungodly hour."

"Yes, sir," Joe responded.

"I bet you're going hunting. Am I right?"

"Yes, sir, and with my wife's permission."

"Well, the good news is, the suspects were reported to be heading in the opposite direction from where you're going."

"That's what I heard last night. Otherwise, I wouldn't be out here at this time of the morning. Evelyn would've never allowed it," Joe admitted.

As he started to drive away, he was offered one last word of advice by the tired officer. "Be careful, Mr. Tanner."

When he pulled away, Joe looked in his rear view mirror and saw Wilson's face, glowing like a crimson ghost in the red tail

17

lights. A little further down the road, he slowly passed under the protective illumination of the last three street lamps at the edge of Grandville. With the comfort of the city lights fading behind him, Joe looked ahead into the thick blackness of the pre-dawn countryside...and shivered at the thought of entering the woods that morning by himself.

CHAPTER THREE

One hour passed and the bell inside the hunter's head sounded to begin the search for the deer. Joe stood to his feet, stretched like a waking house cat, and began the dismount process. First, he took the waist bag off the tree limb where it had been hanging and buckled it back onto his trim waist. Then he lowered his bow and quiver to the ground. He unbuckled his safety belt, carefully put his weight onto the top screw in step, then successfully descended the eighteen feet.

After detaching his bow from the pull up rope, he turned to face the grim challenge of recovering the deer. He carefully walked over to the area where the buck had stood broadside just over an hour earlier, and peered into the leaves, looking for the bright colored arrow fletching. "Ah-ha!" Joe whispered excitedly when, just four steps away, he saw a mere inch or so of the neon green plastic, glowing like a beacon among the mix of brown and rust colored leaves. His hand shook as he pulled the arrow out of the soft dirt beneath the leafy, autumn blanket. He held the aluminum shaft at eye level and there it was...dried, red blood! That sight always sent a chill up Joe's spine. Joy and sorrow mingled. He felt joy in knowing that his arrow had found its mark, but he sensed a sorrow in knowing that he had inflicted such pain on an animal so awesome. The two feelings were never separated in Joe's heart, and he knew the day they were, he should never go hunting again.

For nearly thirty minutes, he slowly followed a trail of blood drops and torn up forest floor. He marked every find of blood by tying a four inch portion of the pink ribbon to nearby branches. Finally, he looked back through the woods at the line of pink that was formed by his markers, and it revealed that the deer had run straight away for about sixty yards, then turned slightly to the right, and headed downhill toward a cedar thicket.

Joe's experience with the tracking process demanded that he not get anxious. Still, he struggled to maintain his composure. He knew there was plenty of daylight remaining, and there was no need to hurry, except for the fact that he had told Evelyn he'd be home by 11 a.m. to complete an important item on her " honey-do" list.

Ten yards ahead was a sign that the buck was slowing. It appeared that it had laid down for a moment. However, the strong animal had somehow managed to stand up and walk on. Joe talked to himself. "Stay calm! Don't break the rules! Be smart, keep your eyes to the ground, and think *red!!*"

With his face to the earth, and bent over like an inspector with a magnifying glass, Joe took another seven or eight steps. When he stood upright to rest his back, his heart leaped when he looked ahead into the woods about twenty yards. First, he saw the dark brown fur, then he saw one side of a twenty two inch spread hovering parallel to the ground. As he knocked an arrow, he watched the deer for a moment to check for the rise and fall of its ribcage. Though it seemed that the buck was down for good, to be safe, he came to full draw, and gingerly stepped forward.

As he walked up to the deer, his first guess was 160-170 pounds. "What an animal!!" Joe said out loud. Confident that the deer had expired, he relaxed his draw. Then, a great sense of relief filled his mind with the realization that recovery had been accomplished, and there would be no need to return after dark with a lantern to track the deer. Joe had been through enough all night searches for wounded animals to teach him to stay out of trouble when it came to shooting and tracking a whitetail.

His mature skills, which yielded the ten point buck that laid at his feet, were a product of his early years spent in the woods with his dad and uncles as they schooled him in the art of hunting. Joe's dad was well known in the area for his record book, non-typical whitetail that hung on the wall at Jim's Quickmart on the east side of town. It sported 27 points, and proudly held a place in the Boone & Crockett record book. The mount attracted both tourists and good business for Jim's market, especially in the fall of the year when the "deer season juices" started to flow in the hunter's hearts. After his dad lost a battle with cancer at a young age of 62, Joe memorialized him as a local hero of the woods by hanging a plaque, and his picture, beneath the large mount. The inscription read,

Taken by JOSEPH M. TANNER, Sr.
27 points / Nov. 16th, 1964
Largest deer ever taken in Giles County

As the 10 o'clock hour arrived in the Gleason woods, Joe knelt on one knee next to the big buck and took a moment to admire his prize. As he did, he thought of a speech his father had given him one morning while driving in an old Chevy pick-up to a nearby farm to deer hunt. With both hands on the wheel, and bouncing in the seat as the old truck rolled over the bumpy, dirt road, Joe's dad began to pass along his whitetail wisdom to his attentive son. "If you're gonna find a deer, you have to think like a deer. Watch him and learn his habits. Get a good idea of what his next move will be. Use every hunt to learn more about the animal. Let your failures teach you how to be successful."

His dad continued, "Remember, a deer always feels hunted. Why do you think their heads bob up and down when they're feed-ing? It's because they don't trust anything. They always assume there's danger nearby. It's in their nature, and that's why they can live so long. The more caution, the more years. Also, a deer can be patient. He can out wait you. They don't have to hurry home...or

hurry to anywhere. They're home already. They just wander back and forth from their kitchen to their bedroom. They don't have deadlines. They'll wait for you to move. Humans can't stand to be motionless for very long, and it just seems like the whitetail knows it. He'll let you make the mistake!"

"Son," Joseph, Sr. went on, "just imagine being hunted. I guarantee you, you'll learn to be alert. Surviving is a deer's job. In order to outsmart him, you have to utilize his distractions, and there's two things that can cause a buck to forget his cautious nature. One is his belly. They love to eat. They not only like the taste of corn and acorns and such, they know they have to store up for the long winter. So we hunt their belly in the early part of the season. Then, later on in the year, when 'love' begins to call, a buck forgets about his belly and thinks about his..."

Joe's dad couldn't bring himself to explain the sex drive that takes over the buck's ability to think clearly. He stumbled over a few unfinished words and finally said to his youthful and innocent son, "Just keep this in mind, young man, if you're not careful, chasin' girls can sometimes give you a lot of trouble! You'll know what I mean in a few years!"

Joe smiled as he thought of how modest and tender his father was, yet how tough he had been when he needed to be strong. His heart was saddened at the thought that his dad could not see the ten point that laid at his feet. Suddenly, a breeze of divine joy swept through Joe's heart, as he thought, "Then again... perhaps he *does* see this trophy!"

CHAPTER FOUR

Ahead of Joe was a process that, at one time, was his least favorite part of the hunt. He remembered when his dad and uncles referred to it as "gutting" the deer. However, with political correctness being an issue, it sounded better to call it "field dressing" the animal. Either way he said it, Joe knew it would be a messy, smelly affair. The one thing that redeemed the unpleasant chore in his mind was imagining the tasty dish that Evelyn could create out of the carefully processed meat that the deer would yield.

With his very sharp, single blade knife, Joe made a long cut beneath the skin of the deer's underside. His blaze orange, plastic gloves protected his hands and arms from the bloody mess as he reached in to remove the entrails. Suddenly, a cold chill shivered his body at the thought of what a Giles County hunter had experienced the year before during archery season. He had taken a large doe and searched the woods thoroughly for his arrow, but didn't find it...until the moment he was doing exactly what Joe was about to do. The front part of the shaft had broken off in the deer's lung area, leaving the razor sharp broadhead inside. When the man drug his palm across the three blades, it cut his hand so severely that he nearly lost usage of it. Joe decided it was better to be safe than severed, so, before continuing the process, he removed the used arrow from the quiver, and checked to see that all the blades were still mounted to it.

Satisfied that it was safe to continue, he completed the task at hand. Joe couldn't help but anticipate Evelyn's standard reaction when he delivered the deer to his home. He knew she would put both hands on her hips and take a stance like a pioneer woman might have taken as she looked across an ancient prairie. Then she would say in a primitive style, "You kill! Me cook!" He couldn't wait to hear it. However, to experience her verbal reward, Joe had to take on the most strenuous part of harvesting a deer. It was unavoidable, he had to get the animal to his truck. Worst of all, he had no help. Hunting alone was not Joe's preference, especially when there was dragging to be done. Fortunately, the big buck had fallen a tolerable distance from the unpaved county road where his truck awaited. Also, his heart was happy to realize that the drag would be downhill a good part of the way.

After fifteen minutes of vigorous pulling on the limp body of the heavy buck, and several rest stops later, Joe was within twenty-five yards of the road. He left the deer inside the edge of the woods and stepped into the open lane, turned right, and began the quarter mile walk to his pick-up.

The late model, full size truck was, as his two teenage daughters put it, "his four wheeled friend." It was indeed a welcomed sight as he rounded the bend in the road a few minutes later. His old '84 truck didn't have the luxuries that his new one sported. He was especially grateful for the king cab that provided so much space behind his driver's seat. There, he was able to store important items, such as his spare bow and an extra quiver full of arrows, without worrying about the weather.

Joe lowered the tailgate, turned around, and sat down. When his aching back and tired muscles felt the much needed rest, he moaned with a sigh of relief. As he wiped away the salty sweat that ran down his forehead, he facetiously whispered to himself, "Deer hunting is hard work, but somebody has to do it!" He thought of how many of his friends at the aluminum plant where he worked would have loved to have been where he was at that moment. Feeling quite blessed with the hunt he had enjoyed, he removed his waist bag and laid it aside. He put his bow on top of its unopened soft case in the truck bed and closed the gate. What a happy sound it was to his ears when the new 8-cylinder engine roared to life. With his mission nearing completion, Joe turned the truck around and headed down the gravel road to his waiting trophy.

On the short drive to the deer, Joe began to wonder how he would get the big bodied animal up into the bed of his truck. As the air conditioner offered a momentary reprieve from the mid-day autumn warmth, he decided to just enjoy the challenge, and try to keep it from permanently injuring his back. He was happy, however, to have the problem that lay ahead.

As he backed the blue and white four-wheel drive to the spot where he had left the deer, Joe remembered the buck was yet to be tagged. It was a detail he was ashamed to have forgotten. He felt safe in leaving the deer where it was, since only a few folks were allowed to hunt the area. Still, he was not one to forget too many steps in the process. He also realized he had not called home on his cellular and touched base with Evelyn. It was a rigid routine he had developed that his wife deeply appreciated, since hunting did have its dangers. Assuming he was just a few short minutes from leaving, he decided to wait and make the call after the deer was loaded and tagged, and while he was rolling toward the game checking station.

Joe turned off the motor and opened the door. Out of habit, he pulled the keys from the ignition and slipped them into his right pants pocket. Then he put on his gloves that were rubber beaded in the palms and walked to the large deer, grabbed it by the antlers, and happily grunted as he drug it the few remaining yards to the bed of the truck.

The four-wheel drive chassis made the tailgate look like it was two stories off the ground as Joe stood over the huge deer and surveyed the challenge ahead. "I'll never get this critter in the bed of

this truck by myself!" Joe mumbled. However, he was not about to be defeated. So, he muscled the head of the buck onto the tailgate, and the rest of the deer's body dangled onto the ground. As he held it in place for a moment and planned his next move, he was surprised by a voice that came from nearby. "Looks like you could use some help, mister!"

Joe felt a little embarrassed that another hunter had caught him in the midst of an attempt to seriously impair himself, so he didn't look up, but responded, "Yes, sir. Your timing is perfect!"

Then a second voice added, "Yeah, he'll be *glad* we came along!"

As Joe lowered the heavy head and rack of antlers back onto the ground, he peered around his truck to see his unexpected visitors. Their faces were not familiar, but Joe was not about to refuse help from anyone at that point. One of the men was dressed in old blue jeans and a well worn army camo type jacket. He had a mustache and a thin strip of dark beard that ran downward from the center of his lower lip, and under his chin. The other had a brown leather, waist length coat with big pockets, and dark colored jeans. Both were wearing baseball caps and dingy tennis shoes. Their hair seemed unkempt and oily.

Joe was a little puzzled at their attire and began to mentally assess the reason for their presence. "Were they hunters?" he wondered to himself, but immediately dismissed that possibility since they were without archery equipment. "Perhaps these guys are power company employees out here working on the..."

Joe suddenly stopped in mid-thought. He swallowed hard and his blood ran cold. His heart began to pound in his chest with a rhythm faster than any deer's presence had ever generated. His hands began to shake. He knew who the two men were...somehow he just knew!

CHAPTER FIVE

"So, you gonna let us help you load that deer?" one of the men asked.

Thinking quickly of a diversionary response, and hopefully saying it with a convincing tone, Joe replied, "Well, I appreciate your offer, but my buddy, L.D., is not too far away. He can help me get the job done. I wouldn't want you guys to get your clothes all messy or anything."

Joe's hopes that the two unwelcome strangers, who had somehow found their way to the Gleason farm, would assume that he was not alone, and that L.D. was coming out of the woods soon to join him. Joe reasoned that his friend was actually one quick phone call away on the cellular, and that he could put his ploy in the "being wise as a serpent" category. His hopes were shattered when one of the men, who's name was Jack, said to his partner, "Man, I think you're lookin' at our ticket back to the big city!"

At those words, Joe didn't hesitate. Seeing that they had no weapons in hand, he suddenly wheeled around on his heels, ran into the woods, and disappeared into the dense brush. He left the two men standing there completely bewildered and surprised by his quick actions.

"Let him go, man!" Jack screamed as his partner felt for his .357 pistol. Joe clearly heard the loud command as he quietly fought his way up the hill. He knew the woods very well and was aware that the crest of the slope he was climbing was about 200 yards ahead. He took his steps cautiously, but quickly, trying to be as quiet as possible.

With a smug confidence, the other man, named Shelby, walked to the cab of the pick-up and stood with his arms outstretched, admiring Joe's truck. "Man, this baby's brand new! We can go in style. It's even a four-wheel drive. We'll be able to..."

Jack stopped his partner in the middle of his commentary. "Hey! Check the ignition! Hurry! See if the keys are in it."

Shelby quickly opened the driver's door and rubber necked a look at the ignition. Finding it empty, he cursed loudly, then screamed, "He's got the keys, man!"

"We've gotta find him!" Jack immediately decided. "He can't be that far away."

Both of them quickly reached into their coat pockets and pulled out matching, silver colored .357 magnum Smith & Wessons. They started to follow Joe's path into the woods, but Jack hesitated. "Wait, we've gotta disable this truck in case that moron circles around and comes back here! He might have the keys, but we'll take us a little prize along with us."

Shelby agreed. "Good idea, man!" He reached up under the dash, pulled the hood lever, and ran around to the engine compartment. Then, he found the ignition coil wire harness, quickly detached it from its place, and bragged as he stuffed it into his coat pocket. "It'll turn over, but it won't fire!"

Jack rushed around to the tailgate while Shelby was disabling the truck. He discovered Joe's compound bow with its quiver full of arrows. "We'll disarm this guy, too!" Jack grabbed the bow by the lower limb and gave it an angry fling. It sailed like a boomerang into the high weeds on the opposite side of the gravel road.

The time consumed by the two men in discovering that there were no keys in the truck, and disarming their new victim's defenses, had allowed Joe the few precious minutes he needed to make it to a cedar thicket where he knew he could hide. He stopped briefly to listen, but his heart was rushing nearly out of control, making it difficult to hear anything other than his own deep breathing. He turned an ear to the road below, straining to catch the sound of his truck rolling away on the gravel. As much as he liked his pick-up, the thought of it being the victim instead of himself was much more appealing. At that point, he only cared about seeing Evelyn and their three kids once again.

Joe had always removed his watch when in the treestand. Once he had experienced the untimely chirping of the alarm he had forgotten to turn off, and once was enough. He reached into his pocket to retrieve it to check the time and when he felt his truck keys, his pulse sky-rocketed even higher than it already was. "Oh no!!... I have what they want!" He could feel his knees grow weak as he also realized that he had seen their faces, and could identify them as well. He assumed that his troubles had just begun. "That's why I haven't heard them drive away! They're gonna come after the keys...and me!"

He looked at his watch and could hardly read it due to his shaking hand and blurred vision. The watch read 10:35 a.m.. He knew it wouldn't take too long before Evelyn would begin to feel concerned if he didn't show up at home on time, or at least call with an adjusted schedule. He hated the thought of worrying the woman he loved so much.

Joe's mind raced through his options as he checked his pockets for anything he might use in the situation that had turned very serious. Along with his keys, in his right pants pocket he had a small Swiss Army knife that had one short main blade. He carried it primarily for the toothpick, as well as the Phillip's head and flat screwdriver for emergency bow repairs. He wished for the bigger knife he had used for field dressing the deer. However, it was in the truck bed, wrapped up in the bloody, blaze orange gloves for later cleaning. "This little knife might have to do me a big favor today," he thought to himself.

In the left pocket of his camo pants were his remaining thirty feet of pink tracking ribbon, and his finger tab. In the lower right knee pocket of his pants he found the long string he used to raise and lower his bow out of his stand. In his left shirt pocket were a black indelible ink pen, his hunting license, and his big game tag, yet to be filled out and attached to his deer. As he stuffed the waterproof paper forms back into his shirt pocket, Joe wondered if the deer he left behind at the truck would ever get to wear the tag that would serve in officially documenting the existence of such a massive creature.

The two felons agreed to shoot to kill as they weaved their way around saplings and underbrush. Jack whispered, "We'll have to be quiet. This guy's a hunter!"

Shelby confidently responded, "We'll find him... and we'll drop him like that buck layin' behind the pick-up!"

Joe continued to wait in the cedar thicket, listening for the crunch of leaves or the breaking of twigs on the forest floor. He hoped the two culprits would not be able to hide their movement. His ears perked up when he heard the crackling sound of dry wood in the distance.

"Man, you're gonna have to watch where you're walkin'!" Jack demanded quietly, as the weight of Shelby's foot broke a limb buried in the leaves.

"I'm doin' the best I can, Jack. What do you expect? Besides... you're not doin' much better. You sound like you're walkin' on cornflakes!"

When Joe figured out where the sound was coming from, it occurred to him that the two men were a sufficient enough distance into the woods, and far enough away from the road, that he could probably circle back, get in his truck, and drive to safety. "This is my chance!" he quietly whispered. He resisted standing fully upright as he carefully chose each step, desperately trying to avoid the snap of a fallen limb under his boot.

Ten minutes later, Joe's thighs burned, and his knees ached, as he "duck walked" his way to within sight of the blue and white truck. He then crawled to a position only fifty yards from his vehicle and waited motionless on his knees. He watched the area carefully to see if there was any movement. When he was satisfied that both men were still in the woods looking for him, he crawled, snake like, toward his pick-up.

At the edge of the woods, he waited another minute and watched the area. Then, as his heart pounded nearly out of control, he retrieved his keys from his pocket and quickly ran in a squat to the driver's side. In nearly one motion, he climbed in, slid under the steering wheel, and softly closed the door behind him. His nervous fingers fumbled in his attempt to slide the key into the ignition. As he looked quickly from side to side, fearfully scanning the edge of the woods through the windows of the truck, he turned the key and expected the engine to roar to life. It refused to fire. He tried again. Nothing. His heart sank when he looked out the front windshield and saw the partially closed hood. Guessing that the two men had done something to disable his new truck, he coaxed himself. "Don't panic ole' buddy. They'll be back here any second. You better do something fast!"

Nervously forgetting for a moment which of the Tanner family vehicles he was in, Joe frantically searched for the door handle. "We have too many cars!" he grumbled. Finally, he found the latch, gave it a jerk, and the door flew open. Before he exited, he once again, out of habit, pulled his keys out of the ignition and stuffed them in his pocket. Quickly he ran to the bed of the truck, thinking he would grab his weapon and head back into the woods. He was surprised and disgusted when he rounded the tailgate and saw that the bow was gone from the truck bed.

Doubt and despair showed no mercy to Joe's emotions as he

thought of having no way to defend himself. Suddenly, a ray of hope returned when he remembered the blessing in the truck's extended cab. "Ah-ha! My old back-up bow!" He ran to the open driver's door, grabbed the "seat forward" lever, and slid the front bench toward the dash, making room to reach for his old bow that was wrapped carefully in a protective blanket. Laying next to it were four arrows, tipped with field points, which he used for target practice. He wished for something more substantial, but since the costly broadheads and inexpensive field tips were interchangeable, as well as more economical for a family man, he would have to do without the razor tipped arrows.

As he pulled the bow and four arrows from the rear of the cab, he caught sight of another item he knew he could use. It was his cellular phone. He quickly grabbed it and tucked it into the knee pocket of his pants.

Feeling sure that his time was much too short before the two maniacs returned, Joe decided to abandon his search for things that might have made the situation more favorable for him. With his left hand holding the bow, and his right hand full of arrows that were yet to be mounted to the quiver, Joe used his right elbow to quietly bring the door to its closed position. He then crouched and quickly ran to the edge of the woods, vanishing once again. At that moment, Jack and Shelby appeared on the other side of the truck.

CHAPTER SIX

With pistols cupped in both hands, ready to fire, Jack and Shelby carefully approached the lifeless pick-up. They had returned to the sound of the engine that had stubbornly refused to cooperate with Joe's attempt to escape. Shelby checked the ignition, and once again, found it keyless.

Jack nervously paced back and forth a couple of times beside the truck. "Shelby, see if you can hot wire this thing, and I'll keep watch."

"I don't think so, Jack. These new fangled trucks are so computerized, it's tough to get one of 'em going without a college degree in mechanics!"

"Just try it, Shelby! What have we got to lose?" Jack said, as he looked up and down the road.

"Time! That's what we got to lose, Jack! There's so many anti-theft devices on these late models, it's useless for me to even try to mess with it!"

Jack kicked the gravel under his feet in frustration. "This guy has seen us! We can't let him see us again, especially in a line up. We'll just have to split up and find him. We'll waste him, get the keys, get back to the bridge, get the cash, and get out of here!"

"Sounds like a plan to me, Jack. However," Shelby added sarcastically, "if you're friend had met us at that bridge last night, like he said he would, we wouldn't be sidetracked out here in the middle of nowhere!"

Neither of the two men knew that less than fifty yards away, concealed in camo from his head to his feet, was a man who was

37

watching intently, and desperately hoping they would give up and leave the area. Also, he was a frightened man who had gotten a glimpse of the two pistols they wielded. Joe swallowed hard in disbelief that he was seeing the same guns that had critically wounded Phillip Simpson the night before.

Evelyn looked at the clock on the microwave above the oven, slightly raised her eyebrows, and offered a subdued, "Hmmmm." She had expected to see Joe forty five minutes earlier. It always surprised her when he came home later than he planned. He was good about letting her know his whereabouts. A few times, however, he had been known to suddenly appear at their back door, two or three hours past his predicted return. She knew what to expect when it happened. Joe would grovel in repentance, then encourage her to go outside and view his gift of venison to the family. Then, he would stand there in a humble, but comical way, and wait for her to congratulate him for his success as a provider. It was a ritual that Evelyn enjoyed, and quietly anticipated, as she looked once again at the clock and resumed her work.

Bob Gleason's phone rang and a voice on the other end followed his greeting with, "Hey, Bob, this is L.D. Hill. How are you doin'?"

"I'm fine, L.D. How are you and your bunch?"

"We're all doin' fine. Summer's hangin' on this year ain't it?"

"Sure is, my friend. But I tell you, drivin' on dust is a lot easier than drivin' on ice!"

"Well, Mr. Gleason, you're always lookin' on the bright side of things." L.D. was grateful that his seasoned friend was sounding strong.

He continued, "Say, Bob, I've got some free time this afternoon, and I wondered if you'd mind if me and my boy, Stan, could come and wet a hook in your pond?"

"I wish you would, L.D. This old water hole needs a good purging. The bass are stunted in their growth. I sure do hope you like brim, too. There's still a bunch of 'em!"

L.D. answered with a thankful tone, "Bob, I'm not picky. I even like tadpoles if they're bitin'! We'll be there in about an hour, and we'll stop in and say howdy!"

Joe quietly took the cell phone out of his knee pocket and nervously covered the speaker with the palm of his hand to muffle the "power up" beep. The battery showed plenty of life, but his hopes that the meter would show a strong enough signal to make a 911 call were dampened when the "no service" message appeared in the small window of the phone.

"I'll have to wait 'till I get to the top of the hill to make the call," he thought, as he once again palmed the speaker, and pushed the "off" button. "I'd sure like to leave this thing on, but as sure as the world, it would ring at the worst time."

As the two strangers stood on the opposite side of the truck and quickly planned their pursuit of the man with the keys, Joe decided it was time to slowly move away from his vantage point and carefully head up the forested hillside. The wind was slight, not enough to cover the sound of a twig snapping under his boots. Nor was it strong enough to mask the movement of the brush he had to gingerly move away in front of him. Every motion had to be deliberate.

"I can beat these guys, I know it!" he thought, as he cautiously stepped over the trunk of a downed beech tree. Then, as high as his confidence soared the moment before, that's how low he fell into despair as the possibility of dodging bullets ravaged his thoughts. He had never been in such a demanding situation. The reality of the danger he was facing was overwhelming, and he had to force himself not to panic. It felt like a frigid December morning in his soul as he shivered in fear.

"God...please help me!" As he whispered the words, Joe realized it was his first utterance of anything resembling prayer since the ordeal had begun, and the comfort that it yielded was much needed. He continued with desperate sincerity. "Lord, you said if we needed wisdom that we could ask for it, and you'd give it! If ever I needed a clear mind, it's now! Show me what to do, and deliver me from the evil that's chasing me. I need your strength!"

Before an "amen" could be offered, Joe heard the distant slam of the truck door, and he assumed the two men were on the move. For a fleeting moment, he thought once again of the deer that laid at his tailgate, and how unfortunate it was for the animal that its life was wasting away in the warm air, all because of the evil distraction the two men had become. It was hard to admit it to himself, but Joe's intense hope for survival had caused his usual concern for the deer to pale. He hated the emotions he was feeling at that moment. As he was hoping he'd see the big buck again, a thought occurred to him that gave him an encouraging idea. "That old deer eluded many a hunter for several years. It's my turn now! I'm gonna have to think like a whitetail! This time, however, those hunters will be surprised that their 'buck' just might be shootin' back!!" As Joe guessed what move the wise old deer might have made at that point, he thought about the cedars, and knew that the thicket which they bordered would be the best place to hide.

Two hundred yards away, and out of range of Joe's ears, Jack and Shelby stepped as quietly as they knew how through the brushy forest. "This coat is burnin' me up, Jack. Are you hot?"

"Yeah! I'm drippin' with sweat, but we can't stop. We've gotta find this guy."

"Don't you think it would be good to split up now, Jack? I'm not too crazy about the idea, but maybe it's the best thing to do. One of us will find him, and if either of us takes a shot, the other can come runnin' and help out."

"Yeah, you're probably right. Since he's not armed, let's split up. You go down the hill and circle back around to the truck. I'll follow this ridge a ways, and then circle back. Keep your eye peeled, Shelby. He's wearin' camo, and he won't be that easy to spot!"

Shelby turned to start down the hill, looked back at Jack, and winked with an evil eye. He gave his buddy a thumbs up sign, and as he began to move, he stepped squarely on a dry, buried, oak limb. It snapped like a .22 rifle. As Jack shook his head in disgust at Shelby's clumsiness, Joe's ears came to full attention, like a buck on alert!

CHAPTER SEVEN

Trooper Wilson was about to turn left on Carter Street when he heard his numbers on his radio. He grabbed his microphone and pressed the talk button. "Car 5, go ahead."

"Car 5," Carla responded from the central station, "we just received a call from a Mrs. Evelyn Tanner. She said she was concerned about her husband, Joe Tanner. She reported he is late arriving home from hunting. She said that you are acquainted with Mr. Tanner, and she wanted you to contact her at your earliest convenience."

"10-4, central. I'll do it right away."

Wilson pulled his patrol car into a school parking lot, left the engine running, and put the shift lever into park. He picked up his cell phone and dialed the Tanner's number. Evelyn answered politely, "Tanner residence."

"Evelyn, this is Trooper Lance Wilson here. How are you doin'?"

"I'm O.K., Lance. You probably know why I asked you to call me, don't you?"

"Yes, ma'am. They told me that you reported Joe is late getting home from his hunt. I saw Joe this morning as he was heading out of town. He passed through our roadblock. You haven't heard from him since?"

"No, I haven't," Evelyn said, with a tone of relief that she was able to discuss her concern with someone.

Trooper Wilson inquired, "How overdue is he, Evelyn?"

"Well, I know it's probably premature to get you involved at this

43

point, but something is bothering me. Joe is very prompt... and he always checks in if he's gonna be late. Right now, he's only about two hours past when he promised he'd be here. Believe me, I wouldn't be calling if there weren't two criminals on the run. It just doesn't add a whole lot of comfort to the situation. I didn't discourage him from going out this morning. Maybe I should have, but with the reports that those two guys were headed in the opposite direction from where he'd be hunting, plus the fact that Joe doesn't get to the woods as often as he'd like, I ....." Evelyn paused in a moment of self blame, and continued, "Well... he's out there! And, I'm terribly worried about him! I'm not ready to file a 'missing person' report, but I did think that if I spoke to someone I knew who is in your line of work, you'd know if those two men were still on the loose, and whether or not I should be concerned!"

Trooper Wilson attempted to avoid the disheartening news that the convicts were yet to be apprehended, and quickly added, "I know that Joe went west out of town, but where exactly did he go to hunt, Evelyn?"

"He went to Bob Gleason's farm. I called out there about thirty minutes ago and Bob had not seen him."

"Does he have a cell phone with him?"

"Yes, he does, and I tried it, but got the 'unavailable' message. I know it's working cause he charged the battery yesterday. Lance, I just have a feeling about this. Can you help me?"

"Yes, ma'am. I'll see what I can find out. Doesn't Joe have a couple of friends he hunts with?"

"Yes. Their names are L.D. Hill and Bill Foster. I haven't talked to them, but I did talk to Tricia Hill, and she said L.D. and their son, Stan, were on their way to the Gleason farm to fish this afternoon. They should be there in a little while."

"Does L.D. have a cell phone?"

"Yes, but Tricia said it's laying on the kitchen counter."

Hoping to steer Evelyn away from unnecessary worry, Wilson offered a logical guess at the reason for Joe's absence, along with the assurance of his professional help. "I can almost guarantee you that Joe is occupied with a deer, and he's gonna be calling you soon. In the meantime, I'm gonna run by my house, check on my family, then see if I can get clearance to head on out to the Gleason farm. I'll check with you before I leave town."

As he drove to his house, Wilson worriedly pondered the call from Evelyn.

As the time crept along, Jack and Shelby grew more determined to seize the truck keys and eliminate its owner. As they continued their relentless search, Joe looked at his watch and realized nearly two hours had passed since he first encountered his assailants. He had endured a long sit in the thicket, and his muscles were growing stiff in his vigil. He thought of working his way through the woods to Bob's house, but since there were two of the gunmen in the area, he wasn't sure which direction to go if he attempted to sneak away. It seemed that to stay put was the best choice. Outrunning a bullet was a game he knew he could never win.

Joe also knew he had to be willing to stay in the thicket until dark if necessary. However, after several minutes had passed, a gnawing need began to invade his senses. With a morning packed full of the strenuous efforts of killing a deer, field dressing it, and dragging it to his truck, as well as trying not to fall prey to a gunblast, his growing thirst for water became an overwhelming, but untimely motivation to move. With his waist pack that held his bottle of fresh water still in the truck, his desperate need for liquids drew his mind to the creek below the ridge toward the area where the dog had barked that morning. He decided that he could stay in the protection of the large thicket and carefully crawl down to the creek. Without water, he was sure he would not be able to last as long as he would need to if it became necessary to run any distance.

Though it was a tight fit, Joe forced the bow over his head, worked it down over his shoulders, and began crawling on all fours down the hill, stopping often to listen. As he fought the extreme dryness in his mouth, he whispered to himself, "Only a hundred and fifty yards or so to go. At this rate, I should be there by next summer!"

On his hands and knees, Joe could see further through the thicket than he could when he was standing. He thought, "It's not as cluttered down here. It's no wonder those big bucks love this place." After another fifty yards of putting one hand and one knee in front of the other, Joe felt something warm and squishy under his left glove. He pulled it back, looked at the palm, and was relieved to find that it was fresh deer droppings. "Whoa, they must be close!" Then, about twenty yards in front of him, he heard that familiar crashing of hooves as two deer bounded from the thicket and ran away. "Oh man," he complained, "those deer are makin' way too much noise. That's not good!"

Jack stopped to listen when the deer began to thunder through the woods. Shelby heard the noise as well, and was closer to the sound. Both of them immediately assumed it was their prey. Though several yards apart, they were still in eye contact with each other and Jack vigorously motioned for Shelby to drop down the hill toward the creek. Before Shelby changed directions, Jack gave him another signal to slow down, and then he put his index finger over his lips in an effort to remind him to be quiet. Shelby returned the O.K. sign with his hand, and headed down the hill, tip toeing like he was walking on hot coals.

Not aware that the two men were only about 200 yards away, but assuming they had heard the noise, Joe picked up his pace and cautiously continued his quest for a revitalizing drink of water. He worked his way to within fifty feet of the bank of the stream, then he slowly stood and looked up and down the openness of the creek bed. Satisfied that it was clear, he cautiously, and quickly, walked to the edge of the water.

As he knelt down on all fours, he removed his right glove and put his face near the inviting pool. Before three sips were taken, Joe raised his head quickly to check the surrounding area. He realized that his method resembled the many deer he had watched as they drank from the same water source. Somehow he felt connected with them in their intense caution, and how they weighed every move they made. He whispered to himself, "deer live like this all the time....*this is life on the edge!*"

Praying that the water was "sanctified," and that a dead raccoon or some other deceased critter was not floating in the water just upstream, Joe anxiously lowered his head to draw one last satisfying gulp. That's when his ears sent a terrifying signal to his brain. It sounded like a sneeze! He didn't know that it was Shelby's sensitive sinuses that had suddenly responded to something in the wooded environment. Joe was grateful for the warning, and he knew he had to move quickly, yet do so without being detected.

The quietest route away from the approaching enemy was up the stream for a short distance and then back into the thicket. Joe stepped into the pool where he'd been satisfying his thirst, and the water line was just below his ankle high, size ten, rubber boots. Three more steps and he'd be in the shallows, and could walk quietly on the greenish brown rocks that were about two inches under the clear running water. "Don't slip and fall ole' buddy," he begged himself. "Take it careful!"

Joe had walked about twenty yards up the creek bed and noticed an obvious deer trail leading up the bank to the right. It led into some thick brush that looked like a good place to find concealment. He said to himself, as he put his camo glove back on his right hand, "Since I have to act like a deer today, I may as well follow their route." At that, he dug the toe of his left boot into the muddy creek bank, and followed with his right boot.

Then, with a strength that came from the "power walks" that he and Evelyn often enjoyed together, Joe bounded up the bank and followed the deer trail that led him into the dense foliage.

Another sneeze softly echoed down the creek bed! Joe wondered why he had heard no voices arguing about the noise. He listened for another moment, then it dawned on him that the two had probably split up. His level of caution escalated when he realized that he had to keep watch in front of, as well as behind, where he was. "Sit tight for a minute," Joe instructed himself. He decided to crawl away from the deer trail to hide and wait. He found a spot where some high grass rose to meet the first branches of some young elm and maple trees. It provided good cover, as well as an excellent vantage point to watch the creek bed. Unfortunately, it was also the home of at least a thousand mosquitoes that were yet to succumb to the long summer. The creamy camo paint on his face, and the tightly woven gloves on his hands, kept most of the bugs at bay. But a few drilled into his sweaty skin as he knelt into a hiding position. He gripped the green and black painted bow in his left hand, removed one of the four aluminum arrows from the quiver, and knocked it to the string. As he surveyed the small opening through which he would watch the creek, it suddenly occurred to him that he was preparing for battle. A dark cloud of dread came over his heart as he placed his finger tab on the bowstring, and checked around to see if he had room to come to full draw.

CHAPTER EIGHT

As he faced the unbelievable possibility of needing to defend himself with his bow and arrow, Joe mentally rehearsed his shot. Although his demeanor would never allow him to actually attempt to kill either of the criminals, he knew he had to place an arrow well enough to disable his pursuer. He felt squeamish at the thought. It was hard for him to imagine what damage even a slender field tip would do to a person, but he was hoping it wouldn't be fatal. Sweat ran off his forehead. He slowly raised his hand, and with his glove, he wiped away the salty drops that were beginning to sting his eyes. "What I don't need now is blurred vision," he thought, as the tension built.

L.D. and Stan arrived at the Gleason farm and stopped by Bob's big, white house. They walked up onto the huge, covered porch and knocked on the door. It took about a minute for it to swing open, and Bob greeted the father and son.

"How's it goin' today, Bob?" L.D. inquired.

"Still alive, L.D. I see you have your fishin' buddy with you."

"Yes, sir, and I'm sure glad for teacher's meetings! Especially when they fall on a beautiful day like this. When Stan is along, the fish just seem to jump up on the bank and put the stringer in their mouth. It's fun to watch. I'm sure grateful that he could come!"

Bob looked at the young man, who was basking in the glow of his father's kind words. "Well, I hope you catch enough fish today to fill up the bed of your dad's old truck. If you need any worms, stop at the barn out back and turn over a few of those old 2x10's layin' on the ground. You'll find a whole city of 'em under there."

Then Bob apologized for the time it took to answer their knock at his door. "Sorry you had to wait for me here on the porch, but I've been on the phone. Seems Evelyn is worried about Joe."

"What's goin' on with Joe?" L.D. asked.

"Well, he told Evelyn he'd be home by eleven this morning, but he hasn't showed. He came out here to bow hunt today. I told Evelyn that it might be too early to start pushin' the panic button, but she said Joe's not one to keep her in the dark. You haven't talked to him today have you, L.D.?"

"Sure haven't, Bob. But I'm with you, I wouldn't worry about Joe. He's probably got somethin' bleedin' out there, and you know deer hunters, when they get on a trail, they can lose all track of reality, especially when it comes to schedules! He might end up being a little late, which I know he hates, but Joe won't let a deer go to waste. He'll show up."

As L.D. finished his conversation with Bob, he wondered if Joe's reputation for promptness was facing some sort of serious trouble, and it gave him a sick feeling. Although the wind was taken out of his fishing sails, L.D. knew he couldn't disappoint Stan by abandoning a sunny afternoon behind a rod and reel. So the two of them headed off to the pond that was 150 yards beyond the big, red barn behind the house.

As they left, Bob said, "Check back with me before you all leave for home. I'll probably have some news about Joe. If he needs some help with one of those record book bucks you all say are in these woods, I'll come out back and give you a yell."

"Will do, Bob," L.D. responded. "And, thanks again for the use of your pond."

Stan added, "Me too, Mr. Gleason. Sure is nice to be out here today. I'll catch a big one for you!"

Joe noticed his hand was shaking as he looked down to check the position of his finger tab on the bow string. To help steady his nerves, he squeezed the knock of the arrow with the inside of his index and middle fingers. As he did, he realized he was yet to complete a ritual he invariably followed when his hunts began each morning. He always liked to get seated, then pull his bow to full draw to check for any unusual problems, such as sight pins that may have fallen out of position, or sounds that might have developed that would spook a deer. As a result of his careful planning, it had been a long time since he'd had a problem in the moment of truth when a deer was coming into shooting range. He wanted desperately to complete the same ritual as he watched the creek bed, but he knew it was too late to be moving around and risking detection by the approaching gunman. He would have to trust that his spare bow had remained in good working order, even after several days under his truck seat in the dry heat. His confidence level was not as high as he would have liked it to be. He quietly whispered a prayer. "God, I hope I don't have to use this thing, but if I do, please guide the shot!"

Shelby found the creek bed and followed the edge of it, stepping as carefully as possible in the soft grass that lined the stream. He came to the spot where Joe had dropped out of the cedar thicket and into the creek bed just minutes before. He started to step between a young maple tree and a large oak, and as he did, he encountered a low hanging spider web. It was a masterpiece of evil proportions. Shelby's face was suddenly covered with the micro thin silver threads. He immediately began sputtering and wiping his face with disgusted vigor. Joe heard the commotion and knew his assailant was only a few yards downstream. His heart raced with fear.

Shelby decided it would be safer to walk in the creek where it seemed to be void of the spider traps. When he stepped in, he gasped as the cold water suddenly soaked through his right tennis shoe. He stood there for a moment to try to get used to the icy, spring fed pool. As he looked up and down the creek, his eyes fell on a brown, swirling trail of mud that drifted toward his feet on top of the water. Unknowingly, Joe had stirred up the silt on the floor of the creek a few moments earlier and unfortunately, it didn't go unnoticed. Shelby's eyes bugged as he realized how close he must have been to his target. He started to yell for Jack, but avoided the noise. Instead, he decided to go solo after the truck keys they both wanted so badly.

Holding his heavy pistol in both hands with his right index finger on the trigger, and both arms straight out at shoulder level, Shelby took slow, deliberate steps. He moved his arms in wide sweeping fashion, pointing the gun to one side of the creek, then to the other.

By then, Jack had worked his way to a vantage point where he could look down and see Shelby sneaking up through the water around the rocks and fallen tree trunks that laid along the banks. He could tell that his partner was on to something, so he dropped to one knee, and anxiously observed Shelby's actions. Jack licked his lips in anticipation that their chase would soon be over.

Trooper Wilson quickly backed out of his driveway, and as he sped off down the street, he radioed, "This is car 5 to central."

"10-4, car 5, this is central."

"I'm leaving my residence, Carla. Have you heard anything from the Tanners?"

"Negative, Wilson."

"10-4. I'd like to get clearance to run out to the Gleason farm. Could you do that for me?"

"Will do," she answered. "I'll get right back to you."

As officer Wilson waited for Carla's response to his request, he decided to call Evelyn as he had promised. "Hello, Evelyn. This is Trooper Wilson again. Have you heard from your deer hunter yet?"

"No," came her soft but worried response.

Wilson could detect the weakness in her voice. It was disconcerting to him and he tried to calm her. "Well, I'm headed out to the Gleason place even as we speak." He knew he was offering her hope without first receiving permission from central to divert his duties to the other side of the county. However, he couldn't stand the thought of not being able to give Evelyn the comfort of knowing that someone was helping her put legs on her concerns. As he turned onto Main Street and headed toward Bob's neck of the woods, he was relieved when the radio delivered the announcement, "Base to Wilson, you have a go to the Gleason farm."

"Excuse me, Evelyn, I need to respond to this call for a moment." Wilson put his phone on the dash, reached for his mic, and acknowledged Carla's announcement.

"Uh...10-4, Carla. I'm on line now with Mrs. Tanner, I'll inform her that she can call you if she needs to contact me."

Wilson returned to the cellular phone. "Evelyn?"

She answered, "I heard, and I'm so grateful for your help. I'll call your station just as you said if I need to get in touch with you. But please, keep me posted on anything you find out, will you? I'm telling you, something is not right!" Evelyn continued with a question she was afraid to ask. "Have you heard any more about where those two fellows went that wounded Mr. Simpson last night?"

Wilson wished he could have offered Evelyn some good news. "No, I haven't, but I can't imagine them being anywhere near Joe. They just vanished and I trust that they're well out of this area by now. We're following every lead, and so far, none of them have taken us to the west end of the county, so don't let that concern you.

"I'll try not to, Lance, but I hope you're right. Thank you so much for calling." Her eyes turned to the clock on her microwave that told her that her husband was now nearly three hours late in coming home.

CHAPTER NINE

Evelyn pushed the "off" button on her portable phone after say-ing good bye to Trooper Wilson, but she didn't put it in its cradle. Instead, she dialed Bill Foster's number, hoping he was home, and that he had heard from Joe.

"Hello," came a sweet, young female voice on the other end.

"Is this Shelly?"

"Yes, ma'am."

"Hi, Shelly. This is Evelyn Tanner. How's homeschool?"

"Really fine. I didn't think I would like it, but it's great! Mom's a good teacher. She makes it fun."

"I know you'll do well, Shelly," Evelyn responded, and then quickly asked, "Is your Papa there today?"

"No, ma'am, he's still at work, but Mama's here. I'll get her for you. Hold on."

As Shelly, the youngest of Bill and Donna's four children, went to get her mother, Evelyn felt a troubling despair swelling in her emotions. She wanted to strike out for the Gleason farm, but the thought of leaving their three teenagers an empty house to come home to after school kept her from going through with it. "Besides," she argued with her intuition, "this is probably just one of those times I'll get to hear Joe apologize over and over again."

"Hello, Evelyn, this is Donna. It's nice to hear from you. What's goin' on at the Tanner place today?"

"Well, I don't know if I should be worrying yet or not, but I'm concerned about Joe."

"Why? Is he sick?" Donna quickly asked.

55

"No, but I think I'd feel better right now if he was. He went hunting this morning out at the Gleason farm. He told me he'd be back by eleven, but he's not home yet, and I was wondering if you or Bill had heard from him."

"Evelyn, it's only 2 o'clock. You know those guys. They..." Donna stopped in mid-sentence and paused as she reconsidered her thoughts. "Well, I do have to say that Joe is a rare one. You know how Bill and L.D. are always kidding him about how bad he makes them look in the 'considerate husband' department. I know your man would rarely, if ever, make you wonder where he is. I've just kind of given up on Bill. If he comes home alive, I'm happy!"

"I know it's probably silly to be so concerned right now, but Donna, I just have a feeling something is not right." Evelyn continued with a convincing tone, "I'm sure you're aware of what happened last night at Harper's Store. Those two guys escaped, you know! I talked to Trooper Lance Wilson and he confirmed what we heard last night on the news, that they were headed in the opposite direction from the Gleason place. I hated to discourage Joe from going out this morning, but it seemed safe to me. Now, I'm not so sure."

Donna felt uneasy. "I talked with Bill around noon about the incident, and he seemed to think they probably left the area, but for me to keep our doors locked and curtains pulled. You and I both know that there are a lot of back roads around this county. They could've circled and gone about any direction. How's that for comforting a friend?!"

"That's O.K. Donna. You're absolutely right about the roads in Giles county. I've been all up and down them with Joe looking at field edges for deer. He has a real gift for making me believe we're going on some romantic evening drive through the country. He always has a gleam in his eye as we slowly creep along those back roads, but I'm not a dummie, I know the word 'dear' is spelled two different ways! But you're right, those two crazies could be any-where out there."

"Bill should be home from work a little early today. As soon as he comes in, I'll see if he knows anything, or has heard from Joe. Keep me posted, Evelyn. I'll also pray about this. I appreciate you letting me know what's going on."

Evelyn told Donna good bye and hung up her phone. As she did, she realized that in all the energy she was expending to fret over Joe, she had forgotten to make the situation a serious matter of prayer. She leaned against the island of counters in her kitchen and stared worriedly out the window into her back yard. She could see Joe's 3D deer target standing next to the fence in front of a tall stack of hay bails. After a long sigh, she began to softly whisper a very timely prayer for her husband that reverberated in Heaven.

Jack decided to stay where he was and watch Shelby as he slow-ly walked up the creek bed. He nervously chewed on his lower lip. "He's on to something down there. We're about to get our man!"

Joe's body was dealing with emotions he had never known before. On one hand, he realized that being the hunter produced one level of concentration in terms of using his ears and eyes. However, being the hunted yielded an entirely different level of intensity. It was much higher. Never had his sight and hearing been so focused. Like an old whitetail buck that bristles at the slightest unusual sound or movement and crouches in readiness to run, every fiber of Joe's being was on full alert!

He knew, without a doubt, that the hunter in the creek bed was moving his way. Suddenly, through a small opening in the mass of leaves and limbs that separated him from Shelby, Joe saw move-ment. He froze solid as ice on the outside, but melted with fear on the inside. He wondered how long he could keep his entire body from quivering under the stress of the ordeal.

The gunman was a mere thirty yards away and pointing the six inch barrel of his silver pistol into the brush on the other side of the creek. Then, as he took the next watery step, with his stiffened arms, he swung the gun around and looked straight at the spot where Joe was crouched in the tangled thicket. All Joe could do was sincerely say, "God!!" It was a cry from deep in his inner being that would've toppled the trees around him if he were able to scream out loud. He also prayed that his camo would blend with the foliage and deceive his pursuer. He could see Shelby's eyes that were filled with an indescribable madness. They were wild and wide, like a ravenous wolf would look at a weaker animal. For a moment, which seemed like a week to Joe, Shelby stared into the brush in his direction, then slowly turned his head to the opposite side of the creek. His arms, and the small cannon he held in his hands, then followed. As the pair of deviant eyes turned away, Joe felt his body relax like a large balloon deflating as he expended a sigh of desperate relief. He knew then that the untrained eyes of his enemy had not detected his presence. Somehow, he felt an advantage. As Shelby was looking the other way, Joe cautiously rotated his head and checked the area above him on the hillside to see if the second man was moving. He was grateful that he saw nothing.

Once again, Shelby turned his gaze to Joe's position, moving his arms as he turned his head. It was as if he were covering his backside with his eyes, and his front side with his gun. It would be a method hard to defeat for Joe in terms of coming to full draw without being seen. He knew he'd have to do it when the gunman's head was turned away, and before he moved his arms. He had to time it perfectly. Otherwise, the outcome would be disastrous. Also, the opening he'd have to shoot through was only about 7 or 8 inches tall, and about four inches wide.

"Use your 20 yard pin if you have to shoot," Joe reminded himself, wishing he could be anywhere but where he was. "Don't overshoot, and don't kill. Just disable the guy, and run! Shoot for some loose clothing. It's tempting to, but don't kill!" Joe couldn't believe what he was thinking.

Again, Shelby looked right at the brush that held the husband and father of the Tanner household. Then his eyes fell on the creek bank right in front of him about six feet away. The water in the freshly formed, soggy impression that Joe's boot had made in the soft, black mud, glistened in the sunlight that filtered through the canopy of the tall trees. Then, with the look of an insane creature, he scanned the brush about twenty-five yards ahead. It was as thick as buffalo fur, but Shelby was convinced that his target was somewhere close.

Joe could somehow sense that the hunter was on to his presence, but was not able to distinguish exactly where. His mind swarmed with thoughts of fear he could hardly control.

Before Shelby seriously searched the area beyond the boot print in the creek bank, he had to be sure of his safety in terms of his back. With the security of his .357 in hand, and assuming he held all the firepower, he used the same deliberate motions as before and turned his head to the opposite side of the creek. Then, the moment he began to swing his arms in the same direction and the gun was not pointed his way, Joe decided it was time to do what he was hoping he wouldn't have to do. He pressed his shaking fingers on to the tightly mounted string on his spare compound bow and quickly came to full draw.

CHAPTER TEN

Joe's old compound bow was in good working order, except for one small dreaded problem that presented itself when he pulled the string back. In the two weeks it had been unused, and in and out of the dry, warm conditions of the truck, it had developed a squeak in the lower wheel. Upon coming to full draw, the bow made a noise that sounded like someone stepping on a loose board in the floor of an old, empty house. The sound shot through the cavernous woods as if it were broadcast through a loudspeaker.

Shelby quickly turned, bent his knees in a police like stance, and fired three rapid rounds into the brush in the direction of the noise. The spray of bullets were delivered about six to eight feet apart into the embankment. The blasts were unbelievably loud. Joe was stunned to the point that all he could think to do was remain at full draw, close his eyes, and wait for an impact somewhere on his body. As the roar of the gunfire settled and Joe realized he was miraculously unharmed, he slowly moved his bow into position to put his white target pin on Shelby. Through his peep sight, Joe could see that the gunman was re-balancing himself from the recoil of the .357, and was listening for signs of suffering in the brush. The seconds passed like hours as Joe held his ground at full draw.

With no audible indications that a bullet had found flesh, Shelby cautiously and slowly lowered his pistol to waist level. Once again he felt vulnerable standing in the stream with no one to watch his back, so he turned to check the opposite side of the creek. When he did, Joe took the needed opportunity to rest his arms that had begun to weaken under the sixty-two pounds of pull his old bow required.

With as much strength as it took to get to full draw, he had to use the same amount to let the string down. Joe was grateful that the wheels turned silently, and that his muscles were getting a break. Though he had relaxed his draw, he wisely did not lower his bow to his side, but held it in front of him in case the enemy was not satisfied that the brush did not hold the man with the truck keys.

Once again, Shelby turned his face back toward Joe's hiding place and assessed the area as the blue smoke from his .357 hung in the air and drifted slowly back down the creek bed. Then, without any warning sign that he was going to do it, Shelby angrily raised his pistol and fired three more rounds toward Joe. First, the leaves and dirt exploded three feet left of his position. Then, two feet to his right, the ground swelled under the impact of the second bullet. The third shot zinged over his head and tore into the trunk of an oak tree behind, and above him.

Joe's ears rang with pain as he fought with everything in him to maintain his composure. He realized two things at once. One, he was still untouched by the destructive contents of the pistol, and two, the gun was out of bullets. Then, from down the creek bed he heard a voice that sounded muffled because his ears were yet to recover from the sonic intrusion of the tremendous gun blasts they had just endured. The voice was that of the other assailant.

"Did you get him, Shelby?!" Joe made a mental note of the name and continued to watch his enemy.

Shelby looked toward Jack, and at the same time, began digging through his coat pockets for more ammunition. He retrieved six more rounds, began loading them into the cylinder, and responded with a voice of determination, "I don't think so, Jack, but these next rounds will find him. I know he's in there!!"

Joe took note of the second name. He also saw that his merciless pursuer was about half way through his reloading process and it required his eyes to get the job done. While Shelby was looking down at his weapon, without hesitation, Joe once again came to full draw. The old bow had healed itself and operated with whisper quiet cooperation. Joe suddenly found himself staring once again through his peep sight at the form of a man. Convinced it was a matter of self defense, he placed his white pin under Shelby's right arm. His intentions were to send an arrow through the bulky part of the large brown leather coat that covered Shelby's right shoulder. He knew the impact could at least knock him off balance and give him a chance to run up the hillside, and escape back into the cedar thicket.

Shelby looked over his shoulder again to check behind him, and simultaneously pointed his gun toward Joe. Then he turned his eyes forward and squinted into the thick foliage. His facial expression revealed a depraved confidence that he knew right where his victim was hiding. "My heart must be beating like a snare drum...and 'Shelby' can hear it," Joe thought to himself, as he winced at saying the name of the gunman for the first time.

Too many seconds were passing for Joe to continue to hold at full draw without beginning to shake under the pressure the poundage was putting on his already tense muscles.

Then, as if preparing to fire at a range target, Shelby cupped the revolver in his sweaty hands and took careful aim into the underbrush. When he put his right thumb on the hammer, Joe decided to wait no longer. He put the small, bright, white pin on a dark spot of Shelby's coat, just under his arm. Still unable to believe what was about to happen, he relaxed his fingers and allowed the string to slide over the smooth, black, cow hair on the finger tab. The bow recoiled. As if in slow motion, Joe watched the neon green and white fletching as it passed through the small window in the brush and flew to its human target. The arrow hit the leather coat with a soft thud and slid into Shelby's upper body. In the same instant, the .357 fired, flew out of his hand, and landed in two inches of water

near the creek bank. He then staggered to his right and fell into the cold stream on his behind. Joe was stunned.

The field tipped arrow had penetrated Shelby's coat just below his armpit. It made a puncture wound that was about an inch beneath the skin and soft tissue of his underarm. Shelby was so shocked and surprised by the impact that he began to scream in fear. "What was that?!!... Jack!!!" The sting of the aluminum shaft, which he had not yet discovered was lodged in his leather coat, began to find Shelby's senses, and he assumed the worst.

Jack saw Shelby fall into the creek, and had heard him yell for his help. However, he was too far away to clearly hear the snap of the bow limbs when Joe took his well placed shot, and he wondered what had caused his partner to suddenly go down. He descended the hillside quickly and ran toward his partner, who was crawling through the shallow water toward the submerged pistol. Out of the corner of his eye, Shelby saw Jack running up the creek bed, and for a moment, he abandoned his search for his weapon, and looked with a bewildered gaze at his friend.

In the chaos created by his shot, Joe took the opportunity to sneak undetected up the hillside through the thickness of the under-brush. For a brief, but valuable, amount of time, he was forgotten by the two men who were noisily meeting in the creek behind him.

Bill Foster pulled into his driveway at 3 p.m., and Donna walked outside onto the porch of their Cape Cod style home to meet her husband as she wiped her hands on an apron.

"Hey sweetheart! How's my fav-o-rite lady today?" Bill greeted Donna, as he had done nearly every day for 19 years.

"I'm fine, honey, but Evelyn's not doin' so well right now."

Bill was taken aback by the abruptness of her announcement. "What's happenin' with Evelyn? Is she O.K.?"

"Well, it's not really her, it's Joe she's worried about. He went

65

out to Bob Gleason's place this morning to bow hunt, and he promised her he'd be home at eleven. It's three o'clock, and as far as I know, he's not home yet."

"And let me guess...he hasn't called either. I know Joe Tanner well enough to know that he'd leave the tree stand with a Pope & Young buck standing under him to make a phone call to home before he'd let Evelyn and his family worry about him. It's just not like Joe to forget to check in."

"Yes, I know that sweetheart!" Donna responded, then suggested, "Maybe you should call Evelyn right now and see if she's heard anything. I'll warm up some of the spaghetti on the stove. Oh...and by the way, have you heard any more about those two criminals that showed up in Grandville last night? Have they caught them yet?"

"As far as I know, they're still on the run, babe. The cops continue to search the east side of the county. That's where they were last seen. I also heard that a truck was stolen somewhere in that area." Bill started loosening his tie and walked up his front steps.

As the two of them enjoyed a comforting embrace, Donna thought of Evelyn's serious concern for her man. "I sure hope those two guys are not anywhere near the Gleasons. Not only did Joe go out there this morning, but L.D. and Stan went out there this afternoon to go fishing. Evelyn said she talked to Bob earlier, and he hadn't seen Joe today at all."

"Well, if necessary, I'm more than willing to cancel my yard mowing chore if my call to Evelyn doesn't bear good news about Joe's whereabouts." As Bill considered the possibility of serious trouble brewing among his friends, the nausea he felt made him forget his appetite.

CHAPTER ELEVEN

When Jack reached his wounded friend, Shelby moaned, "What was that?!!... What in the world was it, Jack?!"

Seeing the multi-shades of brown on the aluminum arrow that protruded from the back side of Shelby's coat, Jack said, "Well, ole' buddy, I think you just had an encounter with Robin Hood. I thought I got rid of his bow. The only thing I can figure is that he must've had another one somewhere in his truck!"

Then, Jack looked around the woods nervously and offered Shelby a chilling thought. "He may have one of us in his sights at this very minute. He's so hard to see with that camo on, there's no tellin' where he is. But I'll say this, we can't let him get away. He knows us. Not only has he seen our faces, after all this yelling we've done up and down the creek bed, now he probably knows our names!"

Jack continued his speech as he looked down at Shelby, then he looked towards the brush where Joe had been hiding. "You were facing that side of the creek when you went down, weren't you?"

"Yeah, but at the moment, I don't want to think about that. I need some help here. I gotta get this thing out of my arm!"

Trying to avoid getting more wet than he had to, Jack bent over and grabbed the arrow near the field tip, and quickly tried to pull it on through Shelby's coat, and through the throbbing flesh under his arm.

Shelby screamed in pain. "Oh!! Man!!...Take it easy!" Jack had overlooked the fletching that prevented the shaft from being drawn through the wound, making the attempt twice as painful. He put his

67

hand around the three, five inch long, plastic vanes on the opposite end and easily slipped the arrow out of Shelby's arm. "Sorry, man! Let's get your coat off and see what damage this thing did to your pitiful little body."

"You're about as funny as a cigarette in a cancer ward, Jack. Help me up."

Shelby removed his coat and shirt and was relieved to discover that the stinging wound was not life threatening, but it would eventually need some attention. "I guess goin' to a doctor is out of the question. But, I gotta get somethin' to treat this hole in my arm. First chance we get, we gotta find a drug store. I don't want to die of some sort of infection!"

"Good grief, Shelby," Jack said with little pity for his partner, "you're not gonna die. I've had worse injuries gettin' out of bed. Just be glad that arrow didn't have one of those razor blade type points on it. You'd really be in a mess. Anyway, I have a feelin' that if that guy wanted to drill you in the heart, he probably could've easily done it. Now put your coat on and let's go find those keys! And...we gotta hurry!"

Shelby held his arm and groaned. The muddy water continued to drip from his pants and coat, and he felt an intense anger rising up inside. "Jack, I want that fool. I have a score to settle with him. Whatever we do, we can't let this guy get away from us!"

L.D. and Stan had looked at each other across the pond when the sound of the gunshots echoed in the distance a few minutes earlier. Nothing was said until finally Stan broke the silence of the peaceful environment. "Sounds like somebody is sightin' in their gun, gettin' ready for deer season, huh, dad?"

"Yep," L.D. responded, while throwing his hook and sinker to the middle of the dark green water, "except...that gun didn't sound like a high powered rifle to me. It sounded a little different. The shots were really close together. Whoever is doin' the shootin' is faster than ole' Chuck Conners on *The Rifleman.*"

"Who's that, dad?" Stan asked his 43 year old father.

"Well, Stan, when I was a kid, there was a TV show called *The Rifleman,* and Mr. Conners played a character that could fire a lever action rifle faster than lightning. He had a young son who was always involved in his dad's struggles to maintain peace in their little town. It was a great show."

"Is it in re-runs?"

"I suppose it is, but I haven't seen that show in years. I wish we could watch a few episodes together, I think you'd enjoy it."

It suddenly occurred to L.D. that his son had missed a lot of the "culture" his dad had experienced. He quietly pondered the thought for a moment and asked a profound question. "Stan, did you know Paul McCartney was in a band before Wings?"

"Who's Paul McCartney, dad?"

L.D. simply shook his head and sighed. "Never mind, son. Just go on about your business. And, by the way, little buddy, your bobber's gone!"

At that news, Stan looked at the ripples around his dancing red and white bobber and set the hook on a nice sized blue gill. He began retrieving it as his dad thought further about the gun shots they had heard several minutes before. While Stan was taking the hook out of the quarter pound brim, L.D. spoke up. "You know Stan, if that person was sightin' in a rifle, they sure got the job done quick. It usually takes me at least a half box of shells to do that chore. They must be good at it, or..." L.D. continued with an inquisitive voice, "maybe they're huntin'?"

Suddenly, L.D. was overtaken by a curious thought that passed through his head, and he quickly said, "Stan, I hate to bring a good time to a screeching halt, but what say we take a drive around to where those shots came from and see what we can see?"

"Fine with me, dad, but why?"

"Well, do you remember Mr. Bob sayin' something about Joe not showin' up at home on time, and how Evelyn was worried about him?"

"Yes, sir,"

"I just want to make sure I'm not missing something here. I want to drive around and see if his truck is still there. I know where he likes to enter the woods. If his truck is gone, then we can assume that he's headed home and everything is probably O.K." L.D. didn't add his worried thoughts about the recent, distant gunshots, and the two culprits that had shocked Grandville the night before.

"Well, let's do it," Stan said with a spirit of youthful adventure.

On the walk back around the barn to the big house, L.D. considered leaving Stan with Bob and going without them to the other end of the farm. However, he knew that if a search for Joe was necessary, the extra eyes would be useful. Also, the thought of leaving his young son and an older gentleman alone without knowing whether or not the criminals were in the area was too unsettling.

Bob was surprised to see L.D. and Stan back so soon. "Well guys, you're missin' the prime time in the fish kingdom. They're just now startin' to talk about their supper!"

"Yeah, we know, Bob, but did you hear the gunfire over on the west side of your property?"

"No, I sure didn't, L.D. I've been downstairs workin' on a floor fan. I had the radio on and I haven't heard a thing for the last hour but ole' Rush. I just came up to take a break."

"Well, Stan and I want to drive around and check it out, and also see if Joe's truck is still there. We just want to be sure. We'd hate to miss something we should know."

"I don't have anything else to do that can't wait," Bob said, with a mature sense of cautious adventure. "Let me lock up and grab a jacket, and I'll be right with you."

Joe was winded when he reached the crest of the hill. He had crawled and duck walked his way for several minutes through the thick brush. Fortunately, he was able to avoid most of the briars, so the noise level of his escape was minimal. He knelt on his knees to catch his breath and whispered to himself, "I can't believe this, I just plugged a human being, I'm being hunted like an animal, I've been shot at, my truck won't start, and my nice buck is rotting! Could it possibly get any worse?"

Jack lowered his right hand into the creek and waved it around in the water to wash off Shelby's blood that he had gotten off the arrow. He lowered his voice to a whisper as he looked toward Joe's recent hiding place. "Now, you said you were facing that direction when you went down. I'm gonna go a little further up the creek and head up the hill side. You go down the other way and sneak up through those open woods, and find a good spot to hide. I don't think you want to get into that thicket there, not in your condition. But what I'll do is walk through that stuff and see if I can scare him out, sort of like a deer. If he comes out, shoot him... and don't miss!...And, don't shoot me, whatever you do!"

Shelby started to walk away, but then he stopped. "I know we've got a lot more bullets than he has arrows. One of us has got to get this guy, Jack, and I hope it's me! I want him bad."

"Yeah, you want *him,* but I want his *keys!*" Jack said with an irritated rage. "We both have a good reason to not give up. I don't think there's anybody else around to keep us from doin' what we gotta do! Let's be done with it. This little war won't last long!"

Joe could faintly hear the crunching of the dry leaves below his new position as Jack and Shelby began to move. He strained to hear the sounds of footsteps above the singing birds and other noises that filled the woods. "Sounds like they've split up," Joe thought to himself, as the muffled crackling on the forest floor widened below him. Knowing that the thicket ended about 100 yards ahead, Joe decided to position himself further down the ridge and wait for a few minutes.

Jack headed up the hill, away from the creek about 200 yards, turned right, and entered the tight stand of cedars with his .357 in front of his chest, ready to fire at whatever moved. He stepped over, around, and through more foliage than he ever knew existed. He could not keep from making noise, and his anger was swelling as the sweat poured off his face. "Man, this is ridiculous. We'll never find him in here." Little did he know that by the time he had worked through to the other side of the thicket, and had come into view of Shelby, he had passed within 40 yards of Joe, who had heard the movement.

Shelby stepped out from behind the trunk of the red oak he was hiding behind and walked over to Jack and spoke quietly. "Well, that worked like a charm!"

"Give me a break, Shelby. You got any better ideas?"

"Hey," Shelby reminded Jack once again, with indignation, "we wouldn't be in this mess if you're friend would've showed up like he said he would! Why don't we head back to that bridge, get the money, and find another way out of here? You know the cops are gonna find that old 'coot' we left for dead when we took his rattle trap of a truck last night. If that old clunker hadn't acted like it was gonna break down on us, we'd be well out of this territory by now!"

Jack flailed his hand at a mosquito that flew around his face and looked around the woods. "I didn't think that old fellow would put up a fight like he did. And, who would've known we'd be steered to a piece of junk that had *farm use* painted all over the side of it?

"I have a feeling he's in that mess you just came through, Jack," Shelby whispered. "Let's go through it together this time. I'm feeling O.K. enough to get this scum bag. I still want him awful bad!"

"Yeah, I bet you do," Jack said, as he looked at the hole in

Shelby's coat and smugly laughed.

About eighty yards away and hidden effectively, Joe laid prostrate in the leaves and looked underneath the brush trying to see the form of the man who had fought his way through the thicket behind him. Through one little opening, about three inches wide, he got a glimpse of not one, but two figures walking back towards the long narrow undergrowth. Assuming they were not abandoning their attempt to find him, Joe decided that while they were preoccupied in the thicket, he would work his way through the open woods, head to the gravel road, and run like a rabbit south to Highway 12 about a mile and a half away.

As his pursuers made their move back toward the dense brush, Joe waited for the right moment to begin a quiet crawl toward the road. His heart pounded with excitement at the thought of successfully getting away from the two criminals. At that instant, from below him, he heard the crunching of gravel under the tires of someone's vehicle as it slowly rolled up the road. At the very same moment, Jack excitedly yelled to Shelby, "Stop!...Listen!...Do you hear that?"

CHAPTER TWELVE

L.D.'s red, '79, Chevy pick-up rumbled up the hill with a low, but powerful, roar. As it slowly neared the point directly below Joe's position, L.D. looked across the cab, past Stan and Bob, and into the multi-shades of early autumn colors in the dense hillside. "Bob, you sure do have a beautiful place here!"

"Well, thank you, and...I have to agree. Truth is though, I haven't seen much of the world beyond this place, not that I need... or... even want to, of course."

For a moment, L.D. studied the careful way that Bob said his words. Then, with keen discernment, he spoke to the heart of his elderly friend. "Sounds to me like you've been thinkin' about that lately. Are you feelin' some regrets, Mr. Gleason?"

Bob looked somewhat surprised. "How'd you figure that out, L.D? I thought I could slip that one by you. Oh well, Sarah always said my skull was made of glass, and that she could always see right through my head, and could read what my brain was thinking. I guess you have that ability, too."

"Naw, it's not that, Bob," L.D. said as he rolled his window down, put his elbow out, and rested his arm on the door. "It's the old *from the abundance of the heart, the mouth speaketh* thing. I've found if you listen close, you'll hear what a person is really feeling."

Stan chimed in. "He's got that right, Mr. Gleason. I can't get anything by him!"

Bob chuckled. "I just wish I would've taken Sarah a few places in her day. She always wanted to go to the Holy Lands. I couldn't convince her that we lived on 'em!"

"I would have to agree with you, Bob. There's a sacred peace on this property, unlike I've seen anywhere else in my time. I believe you and Sarah must've baptized this place with prayers. There just seems to be a heavenly protection here. I've always wanted to mention that to you, and also tell you how grateful and honored I am to be able to walk in these hills!"

Bob nodded his head in a gesture of thanks for L.D.'s compliment, and continued his thoughts about Sarah. "We just didn't have a lot of adventure as a couple, and it was really my fault. Every day was filled with the cares of life until finally we got too old to think about travelin'...at least that's what I thought. I sure wish I would've done some of it with her now." Bob paused and looked out the window toward the hillside, and sighed. "But... she made a journey that topped them all. I seriously doubt if she would even want to come back here now. Where she is... it's a far better place. I sure look forward to seein' her again."

"Me too, Bob. I believe we *will* see her again someday. And truth is, a fellow never knows when that day will come. It pays to be ready!"

Bob shook his head in agreement. "Amen, my young brother...amen!"

Trooper Wilson turned left into the driveway of the Gleason home and left his motor running. He opened his door, and with some effort, he wrestled his 6'4" frame out of the car and walked up to the front door of the old, white house. Two sets of unanswered knocks convinced him that Bob was not at home. His concern, however, that the older gentleman lived alone, prompted him to walk to the rear of the house, check the windows and back door, and generally size up the place for suspicious activity. After a complete trip around the huge structure, Wilson was satisfied that things were normal and started to leave, but decided to wait a few minutes to see if Mr. Gleason would return to his house with good news about Joe.

Evelyn's phone rang and she quickly picked it up. With hopeful anticipation, she answered, "Hello!"

"Evelyn, it's Bill... Donna told me about your concern for Joe. Have you heard anything yet?"

"Oh, Bill!" There was obvious despair in her voice. "No, I haven't heard anything...and I'm starting to really get nervous about this. Joe wouldn't leave me wondering about him this long."

"Yep, you're right about that," Bill admitted.

Evelyn recalled an incident that added to her anxiety. "You probably remember our former neighbor's fall he took out of his treestand a few years ago. He nearly killed himself. The same thing could've happened to Joe. He may be out there laying in a heap, unable to move." Evelyn hesitated in her delivery. "....I guess you can tell that my imagination is starting to run wild."

"I can see how you could feel that way, Evelyn. But let's consider the possibilities. His truck could've broken down. Sometimes it's the brand new vehicles that give us the most headaches. Or it's possible that he's got a deer down, and for once in his life, he's actin' like the rest of us numbskulls. He could very well be involved with a blood trail!"

"True," Evelyn agreed, "but he's got his cellular with him, and I know it's charged. He plugged it in last night, and it wasn't here when I got up. It's just not like him to not let me know something...and it's 3:30 now!"

"You got a point, Evelyn. Your concern is mine," Bill conceded, and offered his help. "I believe I'll drive out to Bob's and see if there's any word yet. I'm sure Joe wouldn't want you to be going through this worry. Try not to let the old imagination factory run too wild. Let's trust God that everything's gonna turn out all right."

77

"I'll do my best, Bill, and thank you for your help. Oh! By the way, in case you didn't know, L.D. and Stan went out there to fish this afternoon. Trooper Wilson went out, too. Joe would probably be embarrassed if he knew the whole town might show up out there. I'll stay here and tend to the phone, and serve as a check-in point for everyone. I'll keep my conversations short in case you're trying to call."

"I'll have my cellular, too. You got my number?"

"Sure do. I have it right here on my bulletin board. Bless you, Bill."

"Thanks, Evelyn, and we'll be prayin'."

Joe was fighting the urge to break into a noisy run toward the vehicle that was moving up the road below him. In the very same moment, at the end of the Currey River Bridge about two miles away, a man in an older model, white Chevy Blazer slapped his steering wheel in disgust, then started his engine. As he let it idle, his voice filled the cab with a speech that was heard only by his own ears.

"This is my fourth trip to this stupid bridge in less than twenty-four hours. I should've known better than to get involved with an idiot like Jack Brewer. I knew he was trouble from the start! But...he knows too much about my past to cross him now. After I get through this episode with that imbecile, I guess I'll have to leave this area and start all over somewhere else!"

With both hands in a death grip on the steering wheel, and angrily pulling it back and forth, as if he were trying to rip it out of the dash, the man continued his self loathing. "That idiot's messin' up a great situation here! I love this place, and now I've gotta give it up for some two bit convict. I oughta' call the cops right now and turn him in, along with his stupid buddy. Man, I had everybody fooled around here. They had no idea!"

The troubled man was Earl Potter. He ended the assessment of his unhappy situation with some language that he had once used regularly, but only on the streets of Chicago, several years earlier. In an effort to blend in with the locals, he had trained himself to avoid using profanity, knowing that a foul mouth would not set well with the respectable folks he had come to know in rural Giles County. He was actually pleased with an accomplishment that had required some serious self discipline. Earl had done well in his quest for decency...that is, until Jack Brewer called him about 8 p.m. the previous evening. The call came nearly two hours after he and Shelby had robbed Harper's Store and critically wounded Phillip Simpson. Earl seethed as he recalled hearing Jack's opening words when he answered the phone the night before.

"Hey, Tony, how's it goin' with my old friend?"

When the caller addressed him by his real name, one he had long forsaken, Earl knew the person was from somewhere in his past.

The caller continued. "Hey, man, it's Jack Brewer. You know... the former Mrs. Jack Brewer's husband. It's your favorite ex-broth-er-in-law!"

Earl's heart dropped when he realized who he was talking to. It was the last person on earth he wanted to hear from again. Before his sister had finally gained a divorce from him, Jack had learned too much about Earl's role as a key player in a deadly ring of heroin and cocaine dealers in Chicago. In an attempt to rid himself of his worthless brother-in-law, Earl tipped the police concerning the location of one of Jack's planned drug deals, and the resulting incarceration brought an immediate retaliation. Earl's "business" associates suddenly started receiving visits from the Chicago PD, and the heat was on. He quickly fled from the city to look for a safe haven, and settled in the first place that seemed friendly to a stranger. He eventually became known to the folks around Grandville as "the city slicker, turned farmer."

Earl Potter, formerly Tony Manzana, had managed to slide out of his past like a snake shedding its skin. He bought an alias, changed his hair style, got a "real job" with a construction company, and even was able to force himself to enjoy denim blue jeans in an effort to disappear into the simplicity of a life in the Currey River Valley. However, he knew the return of an old nemesis, in the form of Jack Brewer, would spoil his cover, and his anger grew as he thought about it.

"How did you get my number?" Earl quickly inquired, bypassing any formal greetings.

"Hey, Tony! You have family that I used to hang around with at one time. Remember? They knew enough about you that I was able to put the pieces together, and here I am! Now that I've found you, and it wasn't easy to do, I thought you'd like to know that I have lots of numbers in the 'little black book' I carry with me that represent a lot of people who'd like to talk to you. I haven't passed your new locale around to anybody yet, but I'd do it if I had to. Now...with that in mind, do you think you can help us out?"

With that threat, Earl suddenly felt sick to his stomach. "What's the deal, Jack?"

"Listen, man, my buddy, Shelby, and me were sent to this area on a little business, and we have a situation that came up. We had to pick up a few bucks for our expenses, and some 'do-gooder' got in our way. We had to put the guy down, and now we've got the law after us. We need your assistance ole buddy... and knowin' your history, I thought for sure you'd be happy to help us out!"

Earl's temper flared. "For the record, Jack, my 'history' is just that. I'm not the same guy you knew a few years ago. Just keep that in mind. Now...I hate to ask, but what do you want from me?" He was hoping that whatever was required would not put his life in a total uproar.

"Just help us get out of this predicament, and we'll leave you alone. You got any ideas?" Jack inquired, while his eyes scanned the street from the phone booth where he and Shelby were huddled.

Earl thought of how quickly he had to decide whether or not to end the conversation by just hanging up. To have done so would have risked the inevitable damage of Jack's revenge. On the other hand, he assumed that to get briefly involved with the pair might serve to salvage the comfort and security of the inconspicuous life he enjoyed in the country. Helping the two outlaws seemed less risky at that moment, so he asked, "Where are you now, Jack?"

"We're at a pay phone near...," Jack paused to look around for a landmark, "...a store by the name of Jim's Quickmart. We're..." Jack stopped in mid-sentence. His voice suddenly rose with excitement. "...Tony, I see a car coming down the road. We gotta hurry. Come up with somethin' quick!"

"O.K., Jack, you need to try to get to the bridge that crosses over Currey River on Highway 12. That's about eighteen miles west of Grandville, and it's the best route out of the county. If you'll look behind the market, you'll see a field. It's dark right now, I know, but it's just a level cornfield. Go across it right behind the store and you'll see a house about a quarter mile back there. That's old man Scutter's place. I've done some work for him. I know he's got an old truck, and it usually sits out in his front yard. I bet he keeps the keys in it. They do that around here. Just promise me you'll leave him alone if the keys are not there! Call me back, instead!"

Jack interrupted Earl's instructions, and responded with an irritated and anxious tone. "I hope this is not gonna take much longer, man!"

"Just get the truck and head west on the hardtop in front of his house. Follow it for about five miles until you come to a 'T' in the road. Go right, and that'll lead you to an old dirt road that goes along the river. It's not the greatest, and you'll have to open a few gates, but it'll keep you away from any checkpoints that might be set up already on the main highway."

Jack broke in again. "I'm followin' ya, keep goin'!"

"Just find your way to that bridge. I'll try to time it right and be there waiting for you. Look for a white Chevy Blazer. It'll probably take you an hour to get here once you get your ride. If you don't show up, I'll leave and come back. If you do make it, and I'm not there, park the truck below at the boat ramp, and wait up under the bridge. I'll blow my horn twice when I come back. Just wait for me!"

"You better be there, Tony!"

Earl recalled how much he detested Jack's intimidation, and worse, how much he hated to say..."I'll be there."

CHAPTER THIRTEEN

Earl remembered checking the clock on the wall of his small kitchen and it read 8 p.m. Hoping to give Jack enough time to make the unfamiliar drive, he decided to wait until 8:30 to go to the bridge, and as he waited for the time to leave, he was surprised by some unexpected thoughts of Sarah Gleason. He was intrigued by an overwhelming sense of closeness to the one woman he had tried to politely avoid when he would stop by the Gleason farm. He realized he missed her motherly-like invitations to stay for supper. He missed her friendly smile. He thought of how persistent she once was that he should seriously consider where his soul would live in eternity. Earl was puzzled by the emotions he felt as he poured a cold cup of coffee in a mug and placed it in the microwave that sat on a table next to the refrigerator. After thinking it through for a few minutes, it occurred to him that it was Sarah Gleason who represented the very reason he had grown to love Giles County. She reminded him of his own Mama! He also thought of the tender years with his mother that were sadly consumed by the "bad company" he had chosen to associate with in the windy city of Chicago. How many times had she said with tears in her eyes, "Son, don't you know that bad company corrupts good morals?"

The truth of those words rang painfully clear in Earl's heart as he battled with the decision of whether or not to remove the .38 caliber revolver from the bottom of a heavy ceramic jar which sat on top of a kitchen cabinet. Frightened and struggling to admit that he was scared, he wished he could have somehow called Sarah on the phone, or called his Mama, and poured out his fears, and begged them to pray. As he stared at the jar that held his pistol, he suddenly sensed that watching him from somewhere above were the two ladies who would not agree with him leaving his house, armed with a weapon of the flesh.

Earl surprised himself when he softly whispered, "Oh God, help me!" The words came out amazingly unforced, yet desperately sincere, as he walked out of his kitchen without his .38 revolver. Praying was uncharted territory for him, since he had never really experienced debilitating fear for most of his life. What he did fear at that moment, however, was not physical harm. Instead, he shuttered at the thought of losing the kind of peaceful existence that was free of waking up day after day, only to live like a hunted animal. It was a lifestyle that he felt he'd rather die than return to. As if speaking to someone who was standing in his kitchen, he asked, "How can I continue to hide my worthless past, and salvage my future? Is there ever any real peace?"

Finally, 8:30 p.m. came and Earl locked the door to his modest home where he had lived as a bachelor for the previous years. He nervously headed out for what would turn out to be the first of several trips to the bridge. For once, he was glad there was no one to say good-bye to as he walked off the small concrete porch into the darkness and climbed into his Blazer. When he turned the key to start the motor, the radio came on and the local country station was broadcasting the news about the robbery, as well as the trail of tears that the bandits had left for the Simpson family. Earl knew he was stepping into a deep pool of trouble by offering his assistance to the two men he wished didn't exist. Thoughts of "eliminating" the pair tempted him. He was certainly skilled in that area. However, he had been away from violence far too long, and somehow, he could see the futility of that course of action. He decided to hope for a better way. As he rolled out of his gravel driveway and onto the road that would eventually lead him to Highway 12, and to the Currey River

Bridge, Earl once again was surprised by the idea that had come to him a little while earlier..."Pray!"

When he arrived at the bridge at 8:45 p.m. he drove across it and parked his Blazer at the west end, turned off his motor, and sat in the deathly, dark silence. The minutes slowly passed as he watched the other end of the bridge for headlights. Finally, around 9:15, a set of low beams rounded the bend about a half mile beyond the bridge. Earl's heart began to pound with regret and apprehension. The lights drew closer and closer, and then passed on by. It was not Mr. Scutter's old, light green truck.

The two hours at the bridge passed like two years. He assumed Jack and Shelby had been delayed for some reason, so he started the engine, put the Blazer in drive, slowly pulled away, and headed back toward his house. Earl could only guess at what level of anger would be generated against him as the rest of the night unfolded for the two men he had failed to meet.

Little did he know that ten minutes after he left, around 10:45 p.m., the quiet darkness that engulfed the bridge was disturbed by another approaching vehicle. It was Mr. Scutter's old truck, sputtering and clanging like a Model-T as Jack brought it to a brief stop on the east end of the bridge. Not seeing a white Blazer anywhere around, Jack drove on to the west end, and Shelby asked with a cynical jab, "Where's your so called friend?"

Jack was agitated. "Well, it took us long enough to get here. And, gettin' lost in those boonies wasn't that hard to do. Looks like we'll have to wait here a while. But first, we gotta get rid of this heap of junk!"

Jack and Shelby both opened the squeaky doors of the old truck and walked to the side of the bridge and looked over it into the blackness below. Jack reminded Shelby, "Tony said there's a boat ramp down there somewhere. Let's take this truck down and launch it!"

As the top of the old, Scutter pick-up disappeared under the surface of the Currey River, Jack turned to Shelby and assessed their status. "We've gotta get out of this area. We're just too hot!"

Shelby responded with a tone of doubt. "Well, we're out here in the middle of nowhere, we just drowned our only ride, it's as dark as death, and your 'friend' is nowhere to be seen. Does that sound like mother luck is smiling on us?"

"We've gotta find another way out. If daylight comes and Tony hasn't showed up, we'll just have to walk to one of these friendly farmer's houses around here so we can take from the poor and give to the rich!" Jack smiled and held up the tan colored duffel bag that contained about $5,500.00 in cash. "We'll find a way, Shelby. Somebody will help us.... whether they want to or not!"

"Didn't Tony say to get up under the bridge and wait?" Shelby asked.

Jack looked up at the jet black darkness of the under structure of the old bridge and said, "Yeah, and I'm sure it's a cozy place under there with the spiders...and who knows what else that would like to eat us for a midnight snack!"

Both of them climbed up the grassy bank and ducked their heads as they walked as far back under the bridge as possible. The concrete was cold as Shelby sat down. "It ain't no Hilton, but I'm tired enough that I think I could actually sleep under here. Hey man, wake me up when you hear the horn!"

Jack laid back for a moment on the cold damp concrete. "Yeah, this'll do. I can hear a car when it comes. I'm sure Tony will be here. He's got too much at stake. We just took too long to show up, and we missed him."

Jack sat up, then Shelby laid back and pulled the duffel bag under his head for a pillow. He closed his eyes, and in a few minutes he was sound asleep, snoring lightly with no apparent feelings of remorse or regret for the pain and loss he had inflicted on the total strangers back in Grandville just five hours earlier.

Jack sat looking down at the black water of the river, and for the first time since the robbery, he contemplated the events of the evening. "Two people down. I sure wish folks wouldn't get in my way. I hate it when they do that! I bet we're a hot topic of discussion in...." Jack couldn't immediately remember the name of the town. "Where were we?...Oh yeah! Grandville!" As if the reality of the potential consequences of his actions suddenly dawned on him, he declared, "They'll not take me alive. No way. I'm not goin' back to the slammer...ain't no way!"

Jack reached into his coat pocket and pulled out a Reese's Cup candy he had taken off the shelf as they were leaving Harper's Store. He had been waiting for the chance to consume it without offering Shelby any part of it. He put both discs of partially melted chocolate and peanut butter in his mouth and moaned with pleasure as he savored the only meal he had had a chance to enjoy since they started their escape earlier that evening.

Jack licked his fingers, then put his head back on the concrete wall which he sat against. About thirty minutes passed, and he stared into the night, dazed and tired to the very core of his being. As if in the grips of the "sugar blues," his eyes began to roll back in his head, and he began to lose the battle against the slumber that he tried hard to resist. He drifted off for a moment, then came to again. "I better wake up Shelby. I'm not doin' too good here. I'll let him sleep ten more minutes...then I'll trade places with him!"

When ten minutes had gone by, both of the men were out cold on the hard concrete floor of the bridge support. About thirty minutes later, around midnight, as they snored in harmony, Earl's headlights illuminated the entire length of the bridge for the second time that evening, and he sat with his motor running on the east end. Underneath the west end of the bridge, Jack and Shelby were unconsciously fighting to stay warm as they tossed and turned in the mid-sixties temperature of the night. Earl tapped his horn twice in a set of very brief beeps, and the high mileage Blazer spoke in an unusually soft voice. The two men under the bridge, who were near a comatose state of sleep, never heard the signal. They just slumbered through it, totally unaware that Earl was once again pulling away and heading back to his house, not to return until the next morning.

CHAPTER FOURTEEN

Finally, the sun rose, and the early light found the underside of the bridge. Jack's eyes fluttered open, and when it suddenly dawned on him what a slumbering mistake he had made, he bolted upright, looked around, and screamed. "Oh! Man!!" He grabbed Shelby by his coat that was pulled up over his head. "Bad news, buddy! We've overslept!"

Shelby moaned in pain as he put his hand on the cool, damp concrete and shoved himself into a sitting position. With the other hand he rubbed his unshaven face. "What do you mean, *we!* I don't remember being woke up to keep watch!"

Jack was exasperated for allowing daylight to come with the two of them still waiting under the bridge. "Where was Tony?!! Did you ever hear a horn, Shelby?"

"No! The last thing I heard was you...promisin' to wake me up when you got tired. You must've passed out. Did you hear anything at all?"

Jack crawled out from the cave like crevice where they had been hiding, stood fully upright, and stretched while holding his aching back. "I sat there for about 30 or 45 minutes last night, and I didn't hear one car pass over this bridge... let alone a horn! I must've drifted off." Jack removed his cap, sighed deeply, and ran his cold, dirty hands through his hair. "Now that I think about it, I guess I did hear some traffic this morning, but I must've thought I was dreaming. Man, I'm tired."

Shelby rolled his eyes in disbelief and looked down at the concrete that had tortured him through the night. He shook his head in disgust. "Well it looks like it's pretty early. The fog would be gone by now if it were later in the morning. I figure it's around 7 or 8 o'clock. Let's go up and take a look around. Maybe there's a house nearby."

The two groaned as they fought the pain of having slept on the rock hard surface, and carefully climbed to the edge of the road. They looked west and saw only the deserted continuation of Highway 12. Jack looked east and pointed his finger to the other side of the river. "Shelby, do you see that road down there, goin' off to the left, beyond the end of this bridge? That's the gravel road we finally reached and followed to this main highway last night. It forks about a quarter of a mile off the highway. I didn't see any houses on the road we came down. Maybe there's one on the other fork. We ought to try it."

Shelby agreed, then suggested, "Why don't we stash the duffel bag somewhere out of sight, up under this bridge, before we take a walk. We can come back and get it. It wouldn't be wise to carry this thing around. We'll go see if we can find a 'volunteer' to help us with transportation. It won't do us any good to stay here. I'm surprised that we didn't get a wake up call by the 'badge' last night. They usually don't leave a stone unturned. Maybe we're too far out of town for them to check out here. But sooner or later, they'll show up."

Jack anxiously looked in both directions. "Maybe you're right. Let's see what we can find up that road. But let's be quick crossing this bridge. I don't want to jump into the river if we hear a car coming!"

With the duffel bag secured above a section of angle iron under the bridge, the two desperate partners quickly ran across the span without stopping until they were about 100 yards up the gravel road that went left off of Highway 12. At the "y" in the road, they headed to the right. Once out of sight, and sound, of the main road, they unknowingly fell victim, again, to bad timing. Earl arrived at the bridge for the third time since the evening before, and slowly drove across it. He tapped his horn, waited a few minutes, then drove away when no one responded to his call.

After nearly a half hour of walking, and arguing about whether or not to turn around and go back to the highway, Jack decided he needed a break. "Let's stop here and rest a minute, Shelby. Maybe somebody'll drive by that we can flag down."

"Sure, Jack, this is a regular interstate out here. I bet I've counted at least a hundred cars that came by this morning!" With a good reason to doubt, Shelby added, "Ain't nobody gonna drive by. This road ain't no more inhabited than the one we came down last night. Let's go back to the paved road."

"Use your head," Jack shot back. "After what we did yesterday evening, if the cops came along and saw two guys walkin' beside a deserted highway, lookin' like we do, don't you think they might assume we'd be worth checkin' out?"

"Well, do you have any brighter ideas than actin' like Lewis and Clark out here in this wilderness? Our chances of gettin' away are lookin' mighty slim to me."

Jack sighed impatiently through tight lips. "Let's just rest, then we'll walk a little further up this road. We're bound to find somebody around these parts!"

For a longer time than they planned, the two continued to sit on the bank that edged the road, and carefully discussed how they would explain their unexpected delay to the people that had hired them. After finally settling on a story they both felt was believable, Shelby expressed his resentment of the undue stress he was fighting. "Jack, I wish you would've left well enough alone yesterday evening! We didn't really need that cash. We should've just checked things out, like we were hired to do, and gone on back!"

"Hey, man, those people don't pay enough money for this kind of work. I did what I had to!!... Anyway, what are you complainin' about? You're gonna come out O.K. on this one, too!"

Finally, they decided to walk further. As the morning slowly wore on, they rounded a turn in the road and surprised their first victim of the new day. It was Joe Tanner, a lone hunter, struggling to hoist his heavy deer into his 4X4, and the deadly game of hide and seek began. By the time it had stretched into mid-day, Earl was angrily preparing to leave the Currey River Bridge...for the fourth time.

Tired of waiting in front of the Gleason home, Trooper Wilson looked anxiously at his watch, then looked up at the afternoon sun. "Well...I guess it's time I head back to the station." With his large hands, he pushed his tall body away from the trunk lid that he had been leaning against. At that moment, the radio broke the silence.

"Central, to Car 5!"

Wilson quickly reached through the open patrol car window and pulled the microphone outside. "10-4, Carla, this is five."

"Wilson, a call just came in that you may be interested in."

"Uh... 10-4, go ahead."

"A Mr. Steve Young, who lives outside of Grandville, called to report that he had seen a white sports utility vehicle parked at the west end of the Currey River Bridge last night around 9:15. He said he wouldn't have thought anything of it had it not been for all that took place here last night. But after thinking about it through the day, he decided to let us know. It's your choice. You can check it out if you think it's important, since you're in the area."

"10-4, Carla. I'm not too far from the bridge. I'll go over and check it out. I'm on my way."

As the October afternoon grew warmer, Jack and Shelby's pursuit of the hunter, his ignition key, and his eyes, had seriously heated up as well, especially after one arrow had already delivered a well placed blow. However, the chase had suddenly stalled when all three of them had heard the sound of the popping gravel under the tires of the vehicle on the road below. Someone was entering the "danger area," and was not aware of it.

Suddenly, Joe could hear the two men blasting out of the thicket as they tore through the open forest toward his disabled truck that was about 250 yards from them. Being preoccupied with getting to the approaching vehicle, and finding a fresh victim, neither Jack nor Shelby saw Joe as they ran within 30 yards of him. Once they were well past, and since they were making enough noise to wake the dead, Joe felt it was safe to take off, and ran in a straight line down the hill toward the road.

As he drew near it, he could see the form of the vehicle moving slowly along. Unable to identify it, he continued ahead, hoping he could get to it before it passed him. He stopped for a second to listen, and could tell that Jack and Shelby were still at a full run.

With the road slightly more visible through the foliage, Joe could see that whoever was passing was driving a red vehicle. He knew, because he had stopped for a moment, his timing was not going to be good enough to intercept the driver.

As he came to the edge of the road and was able to see well enough through the limbs and leaves, he stopped in horror at the sight. It was a truck he recognized, along with the owner's favorite bumper sticker on the tailgate. Ironically, it read, *Real Success Is Ending Up In Heaven.* Joe knew it was L.D. Hill's old, Chevy Stepside.

CHAPTER FIFTEEN

As L.D.'s truck neared the slight curve in the road that was about fifty yards to his right, Joe searched his mind frantically for how to handle the impending crisis. Beyond the bend was his own pick-up, and he knew too well that at any moment the two perpetrators would appear. He quickly stepped to the center of the road, out of sight of the place where Jack and Shelby would likely drop out of the woods. Trying to avoid the mistake of alerting them that he was close by, Joe quietly, but vigorously, waved his bow above his head in jumping jack motion in an attempt to get L.D.'s attention.

The stop lights illuminated on the rear of the truck and Joe momentarily rejoiced, thinking that he had been seen by his friend. He waited anxiously for the white lights to come on indicating that L.D. was putting the truck in reverse. Without yelling, he gave the *come back here* signal with his hand, but nothing happened. The truck just seemed to be suspended in uncertainty.

Joe held his breath, hoping that L.D. would not proceed any further. He assumed that what had brought him to a stop in the road was having spotted the familiar vehicle that was backed up to the edge of the woods and sitting there lifeless. Sure enough, L.D. had seen Joe's truck and was distracted by it, but had not looked in his rear view mirror. At that moment, Joe moved to the edge of the road and began to quickly walk toward L.D.'s truck. As he did, he noticed that the cab was filled with three people.

Suddenly, Jack and Shelby burst out of the woods beyond L.D. and immediately turned down the road toward the red Chevy stepside.

Two miles away, Trooper Wilson's patrol car slowly moved across the long, flat concrete surface of the Currey River Bridge.

"Car 5, to central."

"Central, to car 5, come back," Carla responded.

"I don't see anything around the bridge. Anything else happening I need to know about?"

"No, sir. What are your plans now?"

"I think I'll head back over to the Gleason place and check one more time to see if he is home yet. If not, I'll come on back to town."

Wilson hung his radio mic back onto the dash bracket, turned around on the west end of the river, and headed back east to the Mill Creek Road turn off . He was unaware of the alternate route he could have taken to the Gleason farm across Six Mile Road, where trouble was brewing at the top of the hill. Also, he had no idea how close he was to the tan duffel bag that was just below him beneath the concrete floor of the bridge.

Evelyn was fighting her imagination with all of the strength she could muster. Tears waited at the gates of her eyes as she looked at her wristwatch that read 3:45 p.m. She would not allow herself to fall apart in front of her three children who had just come home, and were made aware of their dad's unexplained absence.

Matthew, their sixteen year old son, pleaded with his mother. "Mom, let's go look for dad!"

"Matt, we can't risk being gone and your dad coming home, or maybe a call coming in from someone else about his whereabouts."

Bessie, the eighteen year old, and a licensed driver, spoke up. "Mom, let me take you out to the Gleason place, or go somewhere. We can't just sit around here and wait. This is driving us all nuts!"

In an attempt to divert her kids from doing something irrational, Evelyn said, "I agree, this is torture. You know your father would not do us this way on purpose. Somewhere in my heart, I feel he's O.K.... but he needs our help. Just you three be sure and pray about this situation. Don't let your dad down. He'll show up, then we'll all box his ears!"

Stan quickly sat upright and pointed out the front window of the truck. "Look, dad! Who are those two guys?!"

Bob put his hand nervously on the dash. "Good grief, L.D., those two men have pistols!"

L.D. jerked his gear shift into reverse and spun the tires. The moment the truck started backwards, Joe quickly ran from the road and headed for the cover of the woods. As L.D. accelerated, he excitedly announced, "That was Joe's new truck sitting there...and I'm afraid I know who those two men are that are running this way. We've gotta get out of here!!"

When L.D. turned his head to look out the back window of his truck in order to drive in reverse, he got a momentary glimpse of the form of a man behind him, dashing into the brush at the edge of the road. He quickly looked forward. "There's someone back there. You two, get down, and quick! Bob, lock your door!"

In the chaos of the sudden crisis, L.D. didn't have time to reason with himself about who the third person was behind him. As Bob lowered his head as far as he could, he searched for the old fashioned lock button and pushed it downward. "Lock yours, too, L.D.!"

Stan could see that his dad was preoccupied with all that was taking place outside the truck and he quickly reached across L.D.'s lap and locked his door. He then rolled the window up as fast as he could turn the crank handle.

Jack screamed at Shelby as he darted toward the truck. "Don't shoot it. We don't need another worthless ride! We'll need those wheels! Just get those people out of there!"

Jack looked at L.D. and yelled at him at the top of his lungs.

"Stop the truck...or I'll blow you away!!"

L.D. heard the command through the glass of his cab but continued to accelerate in reverse. However, assuming the person behind the truck was an accomplice, he decided that if he continued, he'd be looking down another gun barrel. He slid to a stop, and when he did, Jack and Shelby stopped in their tracks.

"That's right," Jack loudly called out. "Now get out of the truck!"

"Stay down, guys," L.D. instructed his son and Bob. "I'm gonna use my *Chevy –.06* to get us out of here and go for help!"

At that statement, L.D. dropped the shifter into forward gear and mashed the gas pedal. Jack immediately opened fire on the truck. Of his three rounds that were spent, the first broke the front windshield and entered the seat just above Stan's left shoulder. Two inches lower, and Stan would have probably been killed. The second shot grazed the roof, and the third zinged through the truck by L.D.'s head and shattered the entire rear window. As the pieces of broken glass fell behind the seat and into their laps, L.D. brought the truck to a stand still. "I can't believe this is happening!"

"The next one goes in your head," Jack said, as he approached the passenger's side. "Now get out of there, all three of you! You won't be needing this truck anymore today."

Bob reasoned with L.D. "I think we better do what the man says, ole' buddy. These fellows seem to mean business!" As they unlocked their doors, they nervously watched the two men who seemed to be filled with desperate rage.

Stan was visibly shaken as he slid across the vinyl seat and stepped outside of the truck behind Bob. L.D. reluctantly opened his door, and with his hands partially in the air, he walked around to the passenger side and joined Stan and Bob. The three of them stood there bewildered, frightened, and wondering what was about to happen.

Jack maintained a police like stance with his weapon, just three or four feet from his three captives, and gave his partner an order. "Shelby, come over here and take care of these three... and hurry up! Looks like the truck is still alive. It's ours now!"

Joe overheard Jack's orders and his emotions melted with fear as he wondered what Shelby was about to do. Concealed by the brush at the road's edge, he quietly moved to a position within sight of the crowd that was gathered just about 40 yards away.

Jack's back was to him, and Shelby was preoccupied with moving his three captives to the side of the road in front of the truck. "Get over here, turn around, and get on your knees. Do it now!"

L.D., Stan, and Bob were in total shock at the turn of events. As they followed the stranger's commands, L.D. wondered where, and who, the third person was that he had seen behind the truck. It suddenly occurred to him who it must have been. "It has to be Joe. Otherwise, whoever it was, they'd already be here to join in this mess!"

"What are you gonna do with us?" Stan asked with a weak voice.

"Just shut up, kid, and kneel down!"

L.D. spoke up, "Don't you think the gravel is a little hard on the old fellow's knees, mister?"

Shelby ignored L.D.'s appeal on Bob's behalf and angrily shouted to his captives. "Turn around, all of you, and kneel down!"

Bob's heart raced nearly out of control as he whispered a quick and very sincere prayer. "God, we're facing the devil himself. We need a miracle!"

"Don't do this, mister," L.D. pleaded. "Just take the truck, take my wallet, it's got at least $75.00 in it. You can have it. Just let us walk out of here!"

"What's your name?" Shelby asked, as Jack moved behind him and climbed into the wounded, but working, old truck.

"My name is L.D."

"Oh. So you're the friend of the jerk that nailed me back in the woods with one of his pitiful little metal arrows." Shelby attempted to deny the pain that still ran down his arm from the shot Joe had made earlier.

"What?" L.D. asked, as he looked over his shoulder toward the area he had last seen Joe.

"Oh never mind...and just keep quiet!"

Jack was getting really nervous. He cranked the window down and leaned his head out. "Hurry up, Shelby. That 'jerk' you were talkin' about is probably gonna show up any minute. Do what you gotta do, and let's get out of here!"

Shelby flinched at the possibility of dealing with another hole in his body. He quickly glanced in all directions, then took a wide stance and stood behind the three helpless captives that knelt with their backs to him on the edge of the road in the sharp gravel. When Joe saw that his friends appeared to be in deep trouble, he quickly stood upright, came to full draw, and stepped out from behind the brush and into the road.

Shelby deliberately, and slowly, raised his gun to shoulder level. "You're first, old man!" When Joe heard those deadly words, he found his 40 yard pin in his peep sight and placed it just above Shelby's upper left arm. Guessing the shot to be right at forty yards, Joe said another prayer of guidance for the arrow, and let the string slide over the tab that protected his fingers.

CHAPTER SIXTEEN

The compound bow made a familiar sound in L.D.'s ears. He had never been on the other end of an arrow in flight, and he could actually hear the fletching as it cut through the wind, making a light whooshing sound. Knowing that the target stood right behind him, he found the experience to be intensely horrifying. He took comfort only in Joe's excellent skill as an archer.

Shelby also heard the snap of the bow limbs, and although he was acquainted with the sound, he didn't have time to react. In the next instant, an arrow passed through the meaty part of his left upper arm, just below the bone, and stopped at the fletching. It protruded from his coat sleeve as his body turned sideways and his gun flew out of his hand, landing in the high grass along the road. With his right hand, Shelby immediately reached around and grabbed the arrow by the knock end and slid it out of his arm, gritting his teeth and cursing in pain.

Jack saw that Shelby had been skewered once again. "Get in the truck, Shelby! I don't wanna be next!"

Joe was knocking a third arrow onto his string as Shelby grabbed Stan by the shirt collar. He forcefully drug the young boy to the passenger's side of the truck, all the while shouting words that such young ears had never heard up close and personal.

Stan screamed as Shelby threw him into the floor board of the truck. "DAD!...HELP ME...NO!!"

L.D.'s heart fluttered in fear as he watched his boy vanish into the pick-up in the clutches of the two wild men. Jack's silver pistol glistened in the evening sun when he held it outside the driver's window in his left hand. Then he drove forward a few feet, next to L.D. and Bob, fully intending to finish the job Shelby was unable to complete.

As he came to full draw again, Joe guessed the distance to the cab of the truck to be very close to forty yards. Seeing that L.D. and Bob were dangerously cornered by the gunman, he placed his sight pin on Jack's left shoulder. As fast as the moments were passing, Joe was still somehow able to regret how painful an arrow in someone's body would be. However, the dread of doing what he had to do was overshadowed by his hatred of the evil that was about to be done to his friends. He also quickly thought of Stan, who was unseen, lying on the floor of the cab under Shelby's feet. Praying that his young friend would be unharmed, Joe let the arrow fly, and the thirty inch aluminum "bullet" whizzed by Jack's left ear. It barely missed his shoulder, and came to an extremely noisy halt on the window frame above the steering wheel, then suddenly changed directions, and shot straight downward. The shaft broke in half, making a deafening noise that so surprised and frightened Jack that it caused him to mash the accelerator. Dirt and gravel flew as the truck sped off and went out of sight around the bend, beyond Joe's pick-up.

Like the silence that returns after a thundering tornado passes through, the roadside was quiet once again. The dust hung silently in the air above the road as Bob and L.D. slowly stood to their feet and stared helplessly in the direction they had last seen Stan. At that moment, Joe ran to meet his friends. When they turned to see who was coming, Joe saw that their faces were ashen white. L.D.'s countenance made it painfully clear that he was in complete shock. "Joe, they've got my boy! Oh God, have mercy, they've got my boy!!"

Bob and Joe looked at each other in silent agreement. Never before had they heard more heart wrenching words come from a man. Tears began to fill L.D.'s eyes as Joe put his arm around his friend's shoulder.

"What are we gonna do, fellows?" L.D. asked pitifully.

Joe quickly dug into his knee pocket, retrieved his cellular phone, and pushed the power button. "We'll get your boy back, L.D.!" Joe said, hoping to offer his desperate friend a small ray of hope. "We've just gotta get some help. Maybe this phone will connect this time!" Joe knew he had unsuccessfully tried to get a call through earlier that day, just about fifty yards from where he stood. While he waited, and earnestly prayed for the phone to show enough signal strength to make a call, he said, "Bob, we know those guys are driving toward a 'T' in the road. If they go right, they'll go by your house. If they go left, we know they'll end up below us."

Bob nodded his head in agreement. "Yea, and if they go left, as you know, they'll end up back at Highway 12, just above the Currey River Bridge. Who knows which way they'll go after that?!"

"Ah-hah!" Joe announced, "Hallelujah! We've got a signal!" He dialed 911, pushed the green button to send the call, and put the phone to his ear. As he waited anxiously for an answer, he looked at L.D. and his heart groaned in sorrow for the man who still stared in the direction of his captured son.

The phone suddenly came to life in Joe's ear. A scratchy, broken signal delivered a welcomed voice. "911 operator. How can I assist you?"

"Hello! Yes, I have an emergency!"

"Yes, sir. Go ahead please."

"There's been a shooting and a young boy has been kidnapped. A very serious situation has developed out here in the western side of Giles County about 18 or 20 miles from Grandville!"

"Has anyone been injured, sir? Do you need an ambulance?"

"No, ma'am, just police. We really need the police!" Joe was grateful that someone was listening. "I believe we've encountered the two men that robbed the Harper's Store last night. They disabled my truck and shot at me this morning. Now they've taken a Chevy pick-up that belongs to my friend, L.D. Hill. And worst of all, they have his twelve year old son with them as a hostage!"

"Where are you exactly at this moment, sir?"

"The best way to tell you is that on the east end of the Currey River Bridge, there's a gravel road that goes to the north. Right now, L.D. Hill, Bob Gleason, and I are standing on it at a point half way between Highway 12 and Mill Creek Road. It's called Six Mile Road."

"Sir, did you say a Mr. Bob Gleason is with you?"

"Yes, ma'am!"

"I believe State Trooper Wilson is at Mr. Gleason's residence right now. He went there to ask about the whereabouts of a Mr. Joe Tanner. Would that happen to be you, sir?"

Thankful that someone would ask about him, and that Lance Wilson was in the area, Joe answered the operator with a grateful sigh. "Yes, that's me!"

"Sir, your family has called about you. I'll let them know you are O.K. Now, Mr. Tanner, I need to get just one detail from you very quickly, and then I will send you some assistance right away. When we contact Trooper Wilson, how shall we tell him to get to you?"

"Tell Wilson to turn left out of Bob's driveway and head west toward the next road that goes to the left. That's where he'll find us. But also tell him that he just might see L.D. Hill's red, Chevy, stepside pick-up truck. The windows are shot out of it, and there's a kid in there with the two suspects. One of 'em is armed, but believe me, they're both dangerous. One of them was wounded twice, once in each arm by aluminum arrows. They weren't critical wounds, but neither of them are happy campers. And, please tell Wilson that if he sees them, he must be careful to do what he can to keep the boy safe! Just tell him to play it cool!"

The operator thanked Joe for the information and asked him to stay on line. "Ma'am, I need to hang up for a minute and one of us will call you back shortly."

"Please do so, Mr. Tanner. We don't want to lose contact with you if possible."

Joe pushed the "end" button on the phone and handed it to Bob. "If you don't mind, take this phone over to my truck, and in the glove compartment you'll find a cigarette lighter adapter for it. Plug it in, and get back on line with the 911 operator. Stay low, just in case those guys come back through here. If they don't see anyone in the cab, they'll most likely go on by. My truck is dead, and unfortunately, I have the keys. I don't have time to explain what that means, but it's one of the reasons we're in this mess right now."

Joe continued forming a plan. "L.D., see if you can find that pistol that flew into the grass, then hide yourself and wait along the road here. If they do happen to come back through, you'll have a way to defend yourself. I'm gonna go down through these woods to the road below us. If they didn't turn left at the 'T' in the road, and haven't already circled around and headed back to Highway 12, they'll end up in an encounter with Trooper Wilson, who, by the way, Bob, is at your house right now trying to find out where I am. Once they meet him, they'll probably turn around and end up on the road where I'll be. Let's just hope they turned right when they got to Mill Creek Road! May God help us, fellows. We need Him awful bad right now."

L.D. sighed deeply. "We sure do!" Then he turned toward the edge of the road and began a search for the pistol. Bob quickly walked toward Joe's truck with the cell phone in his hand, and Joe headed downhill toward the road below them. As he pushed aside the limbs full of early October foliage, he whispered to himself, "God, make my heart strong." At the moment the three friends split up, L.D.'s old truck was bouncing along toward Bob's house on

Mill Creek Road.

CHAPTER SEVENTEEN

"Mrs. Tanner?" the voice on the phone asked.

"Yes, this is Evelyn Tanner."

"This is Officer Barton from the Grandville Police Department."

Evelyn gasped in fear of a bad report. "Oh goodness, what's the news?"

"A 911 operator informed us that she received a cell phone call from your husband a few minutes ago, and he reported that he is on Six Mile Road near Mr. Bob Gleason's farm. He indicated that with him is L.D. Hill and Mr. Gleason. He also reported that he had encountered the two men that robbed the Harper's Store last evening. At this time, all we know is that the three of them are involved in a situation that includes the kidnapping of a fourth individual, Mr. Hill's son. It seems rather complicated right now, but along with the troopers involved in the case, we're gonna do what we can to bring this thing to a close."

Evelyn struggled to maintain her composure. "That certainly is both good news and bad news. Is anyone injured? Did they hurt the boy?"

"No ma'am, no reports of physical injury were given."

"Thank you so much for calling. What can we do here?" Evelyn asked, feeling relieved that Joe was not wounded, but at the same time feeling horrified about the grave danger Stan was facing.

"It may be best to sit tight for now. We'll notify you the moment we know more details."

"And we will be praying, too!"

"Yes, ma'am. You would do well to do that! I'll join you."

As Evelyn hung up the phone, it dawned on her that Donna would be getting the same call, notifying her of the situation that had developed regarding her husband and son. She whispered a prayer for her friend as she dialed her number. It was already busy.

"Central, to car 5, do you copy?"

"This is car 5, come back," Wilson responded.

"We just got a call from Mr. Joe Tanner on a cell phone. He has reported that he encountered the two suspects from the Harper Store robbery. If you are at, or near, the Bob Gleason farm, Mr. Tanner said that they are possibly headed in that direction at this moment in a red, Chevy stepside type truck. The vehicle has the front and rear windows missing as a result of gunfire."

"10-4, central. I am within eyesight of that residence right now."

"Wilson, please be advised that the two men have a hostage in the truck. It is the son of Mr. L.D. Hill. His name is Stan, and he's twelve years old. The two men are assumed to be armed!"

"10-4. Any more information?"

"Mr. Tanner said that his position is on Six Mile Road half way between Highway 12 and Mill Creek Road, which is west of Mr. Gleason."

"Anybody injured?" Wilson asked as he slowed to a stop in front of the Gleason home.

"Only one of the suspects received injury from Mr. Tanner's bow and arrow he apparently had in his possession. The wounds were reported as non-life threatening."

Wilson looked left out his window at the Gleason home and all seemed to be well. "Central, I am going to roll on by the Gleason residence and continue toward Mr. Tanner's 10-20."

Carla responded, "I repeat, Mr. Tanner advised that the two suspects may, or may not be, headed that way. Whatever the case, keep the young boy in mind. Also, Mrs. Tanner has been contacted about

110

her husband, and Mrs. Hill is receiving a call as well. We are sending more units to the area."

"10-4, central. I'm rolling!"

Bob retrieved the cigarette lighter power adapter from the glove compartment of Joe's truck, plugged it into the base of the phone, then into the lighter. He stared at the cellular contraption and was confused by all the buttons. The world of modern communication devices had eluded him and he was puzzled about what to do. "Lord, I lack wisdom here!" he whispered as he searched the face of the phone.

He saw the power button and pushed it, and the phone came to life. He pushed 911 and held it to his ear and waited. Nothing happened. He repeated the same steps. Still, nothing in the ear piece. "I'm doin' somethin' wrong here," he nervously mumbled, as he looked at the wide array of options. Finally he saw the word "send" on the green button and assumed that it had to be the right choice. He pushed it, and once again put the phone to his ear. He felt technically accomplished, and prayerfully grateful, when it rang and the voice on the other end said, "911 operator, how can I assist you?"

"Hello, this is Bob Gleason."

"Yes, Mr. Gleason," the operator answered. "Thank you for calling. What is your report?"

"I am inside of Joe Tanner's truck. He suggested I call you and stay on here with you."

"Yes, sir. I will connect you with an assistant. We will need to converse with you from time to time. We want to be assured of your welfare until an officer arrives. At that time, you may disconnect."

"Will do, ma'am. Thanks for your help!"

L.D. had easily recovered the .357 and checked the cylinder to see if it was loaded. Three bullets remained, and he angrily whispered to himself, "I hope I get to use at least two of these before the day is over!"

Along with an intense anger, he felt a growing despair well up inside him as he realized that if his truck came by him, more flying bullets would be the last thing Stan needed. As he stood by the road, he looked up to the sky, closed his eyes, and quietly said, "What we need here is a miracle! God, please protect Stan...please. Give him a supernatural strength, and fill his mind with peace and wisdom. Guide him Lord. Please bring him back safely to us!"

Joe was sweating profusely as he fought his way through the brush toward the road below. He was especially glad that it was slightly down hill the whole way. While he descended the hill as swiftly as he could, he asked himself a hard question. "If they do come by here, what on earth am I gonna do?"

Earl Potter had left his home on Bender's Gap Road and turned right on Mill Creek. He had no idea that he was one minute behind Trooper Wilson. He had decided to go to Bob's house and seek his seasoned wisdom. As he thought of the risky trips he had already made to the Currey River Bridge, he comforted himself by saying, "Surely the old gentleman will help me. He'll listen to me. He'll believe my story. I know I can trust him!"

As Earl came over a rise in the road, and the Gleason farm came into view, he caught a glimpse of a patrol car making the turn in the bend that was beyond Bob's house about a quarter of a mile. His heart fluttered in fearful excitement when he realized that the search for Jack and Shelby had apparently moved into the area. Earl stopped his Blazer in the gravel road to think for a moment, knowing that he faced an incredibly important choice. He softly worded a question he never thought he would utter. "What would Sarah suggest I do in this moment?"

His heart knew the answer to the question, but he found it very difficult to let it find a resting place in his mind. Admitting to himself that the time had come in his life to find a lasting peace, he whispered, "She'd tell me to face the music...and speak the truth! All I can do is hope for mercy. I'm tired of running!"

With that major milestone reached in his heart, Earl decided to chase down the patrol car and offer his assistance in the pursuit of the two men. Unknowingly, at that very moment, Jack and Shelby were moving rapidly in his direction, toward a rendezvous with Trooper Wilson. As Earl pressed the accelerator under his foot, he suddenly felt a level of calmness that he had not felt in many years. Without doubting, even for a moment, where he had heard the phrase before, Earl said to himself in the solitude of the cab of his Blazer, "This is kind of like getting all cleaned up inside!" All the years of living for himself and doing what he thought was right for the moment seemed empty and wasted. He knew it was time for an ultimate change.

As Earl drove off to catch up with Trooper Wilson, Joe came to the edge of the road below Six Mile. There, he found a huge clump of leafy brush that he was able to use to conceal himself. It gave him a vantage point from which he could clearly see five to six hundred yards in either direction. As he panted from the half mile run down the hill, he knocked his last arrow onto the string, took a practice draw, anxiously watched, and intently listened as the late afternoon sun headed toward the horizon. In the stillness of the countryside, he thought of Evelyn and his kids who, he hoped by then, had received the news of his whereabouts. He knew they would be relieved for only a moment, only to become anxious again when they learned of his encounter with "Donnie and Clyde." Then his emotions were suddenly swept up in a vicious wave of despair as he thought of young Stan Hill, stuck in the cab of his dad's old truck with the two dangerous strangers. He wondered where they were, and he offered a quiet prayer. "God, give us peace in the face of this enemy. It'll be a sign of defeat to those guys if you'll give us peace. We're not wrestling with flesh and blood here, Lord. This battle is in another realm. Only you can help us!"

As Joe whispered "amen" at the end of his heartfelt cry, he thought of a comparison between his situation and another familiar story. He soberly said to himself, "If they come down this road, I'll have only one stone to throw at this Goliath. It better be a good shot!"

CHAPTER EIGHTEEN

A few minutes earlier, when Jack had arrived at the intersection of Six Mile and Mill Creek Roads, he barked at Stan. "Sit up kid!"

Stan sat up and looked over the dash at his surroundings. As Jack held the steering wheel in his left hand, with his right, he grabbed Stan by the shirt collar and pulled him toward his face, and demanded, "You need to tell us which way to go here, you little twit. And you better tell the truth. You know this area, don't you?"

"Yes, sir." Stan answered with a trembling voice, and nearly gagged at the smell of Jack's breath. "If you go right, it'll take you to Highway 12 in about four or five miles." He thought about telling them that a left turn would be a quicker way to the main road, but he took comfort in leading the two men on a route where at least he knew there were houses.

When Jack turned right onto Mill Creek Road and accelerated, the truck swerved left and right in the gravel. Little did he know that ahead of them, Trooper Wilson was slowly moving along the same road in their direction. The rack of blue lights on the patrol car would not be a welcomed sight for the pair.

Jack let go of Stan, and Shelby forcefully pushed him back to the floor of the truck. "Stay down, you little twerp! And don't even think about gettin' up!"

Jack angrily yelled at Shelby as the wind whipped through the open windshield. "The kid's our ticket out of here, Shelby. Try not to hurt him! Here...make yourself useful and reload my gun."

As Shelby opened the cylinder of the .357 and loaded three more rounds into it, his voice turned to a wolf-like growl. "This stupid kid must be the son of that L.D. guy. I'm gonna take great pleasure in using this little squirt to make his daddy's buddy, *Mr. Robin Hood,* regret he ever saw my face!" As Shelby said the words, he handed the pistol back to Jack and pulled his coat off for the first time since his second injury, and reluctantly looked at his wound.

"How's your arm, man?"

"Arms, Jack! Arms! Both of 'em are hurtin' real bad. Feels like somebody poked a hot branding iron down in my left one. I've gotta get somethin' to clean these holes! And the blood has ruined my coat. I'm in bad shape, man!"

"I hope those guys don't find that gun you lost back there!" Jack said, ignoring Shelby's prognosis of himself. "It's got your finger prints all over it!"

Shelby looked straight ahead, and attempted to hide his fear of leaving behind such incriminating evidence. "We won't see 'em again. Don't worry about it."

Jack gripped the steering wheel extra tight and wiped the dust from his eyes that was coming through the unprotected window in front of him. "We're in this thing deeper than I intended. But we can't turn back. We may have to go out in a blaze of glory, ole' buddy, but I ain't goin' back to the pen!"

As Stan laid on the floor, wondering what would happen to him, he was shaking with fear. His right cheek was pressed to the rubber mat on the floor, and as he faced the underside of the bench on the passenger side, he felt Shelby's heavy foot on his back. As the rubber soled tennis shoe pressed onto his spine, holding him firmly to the floor, Stan suddenly felt a calmness that surprised him, and he boldly spoke up. "Mister, would you kindly take your foot off my back? It sure is making things rougher down here."

"I said shut up, kid! One more word and I'll hang you out the window by your feet and drag your little, ugly face on the road!"

As Stan's jaw bounced on the rubber mat, his eyes fell on an item under the bench that brought a ray of hope to his heart. He was especially happy that he was the only one in the truck who knew it was there. It was one of his dad's knives, tucked away in a black leather sheath with a velcro latch. It had a four inch folding blade and a composite handle. It was compact enough for Stan's pants pocket, and he slowly moved his arm toward it. Without being noticed among the jostling ride, he wrapped his fingers around the case, and to avoid the "swooshing" sound of separating velcro, he slowly opened the cover. He quietly slipped the knife out of its sheath, and without being detected, he slid it into the left pocket of his pants and continued to stare under the seat.

Another item caught his eye. It was an old, green, nylon fish stringer, about six feet in length. It had a rusted metal guide on one end and a quarter coin sized metal loop on the other. As he slowly moved his arm toward the stringer, he saw before him a grand opportunity in the form of a large loop in Shelby's tennis shoe string. Not really knowing where the ideas were coming from, he thought to himself, "If I could somehow connect this stringer from his shoe lace to this seat, it might help me escape if I get a chance to run. But I'm gonna need both hands to do it."

Hoping that the man who was driving would come to his defense again, Stan spoke up once more. "Mister, would you mind if I turned over on my side?"

Shelby clinched his fist and held it up in front of Stan's face. Jack could tell that the boy was about to get a beating. "Let him do it Shelby, he can't hurt anything!"

Shelby glared at Jack with intense resentment, then stubbornly eased the pressure. With the freedom to move, Stan wiggled his way onto his side, in a fetal position, and it allowed him to reach with both arms under the truck bench. "This is great!" he thought, as he began an attempt to anchor his assailant to his dad's wounded truck. "I've got to leave him enough slack to be able to shuffle his feet without knowing he's connected." Feeling surprised again, yet confident, with the idea, he gradually slid the metal guide that was designed for a fish's mouth, up and over the curled spring supporting the underside of the bench, then slipped it through the metal ring. As the two men above him loudly talked back and forth, he pulled the six remaining feet of string on through, leaving enough length to attach to Shelby's shoelace. With the same care a doctor would give to brain surgery, he carefully slipped the guide through the loop in the lace of Shelby's shoe that sat next to the door. As the truck bounced on the bumpy, country road, Stan fought to steady his hands. Within two minutes, he finally succeeded in tying the nylon string into a knot, and Shelby was oblivious to the trap. Stan then whispered reassuring words to himself. "I'll get away from these guys. I know I will. God, please help me!"

Bill Foster finished putting gas into his big, new, hunter green Suburban, hung the nozzle back onto the pump, and paid the attendant. As he drove away from the station, he called Donna on his cellular.

"Donna, I had to run by the office and get my battery for my cell phone. Plus, I had to get some gas before leaving town. Now, finally, I'm on my way to Bob's. Have you heard anything since I left the house?"

"Yes. Thank God you called. I just heard a few minutes ago that Joe has been located. He somehow got tangled up with those two guys on the run from the law. He's O.K. But, the bad news is, the two criminals ended up with Stan Hill as a hostage."

"You're kidding, Donna!!...Where is Joe and L.D.?"

"I'm not quite sure, except I know they're still out at the Gleason farm area."

Donna had no doubt about what Bill would do, and she had no intentions of trying to stop her husband from assisting his friends.

However, she needed, for her sake, to ask Bill one question. "Bill...
I know you want to help out there. I just need to know one thing.
Do you have anything with you to...you know...?"

"You mean...to protect myself with?" Bill asked, a little surprised that Donna wanted him to have some fire power.

"Yes, sweetheart...I just hope you don't get hurt out there."

"Well, you'll be glad to know I didn't bring a gun. Somehow, I
managed to leave without it, and I really don't have time to go back
and get it. But...I do have my birthday gift with me!".

"You mean you have that crossbow?"

Bill answered confidently. "Yep. I may not have a gun, but I
brought the next best thing. I just hope I don't have to use it!"

"Me, too!...Are you good with it?"

"Well, I haven't hunted with it, but I've shot it enough to feel
confident. I have four bolts with me. I don't think I'll have to use it,
but if I have to, I can do it."

For some reason, Donna didn't find a lot of consolation in Bill's
limited experience and thought of a more comforting idea. "Bill, I
think the best weapon we have at this point is prayer. We can use
our *Cross-bow!*... Get it?"

Donna's attempt to ease the tension with a little bit of divine
humor went understandably over the head of her worried husband,
who simply answered, "I love ya babe. I'll see you after a while."
Donna hung up the phone and sat down on a stool in her den. She
stared out her bay windows, and offered a quiet prayer for Bill and
their friends.

Matthew Tanner paced the floor for several minutes and finally
spoke up with a tone that startled Evelyn and his sisters, who were
sitting at the kitchen table.

"We've gotta do something, Mom!! We can't just sit here. It'll
be dark in a couple of hours and dad's still out there. Stan's in dan-

ger, and here we sit! Can't we do anything besides sit here like *zombies?*"

With her elbows on their round, oak, kitchen table, Evelyn bowed her head and placed her fingertips on her temples. The volume of her son's voice, that was normally subdued, revealed the strain and fear that gripped him. She looked up at Matthew and stared briefly into his young eyes. "I'm with you, Matt. I want to do something, too... anything but sit here!"

"Well, why don't we go? We're worthless here. We know that area around Mr. Gleason's farm. Maybe we could help the police navigate it!"

Evelyn was suspended in the vast space between sitting like a slug at home and going off to conquer the enemy. Although she was not at all sure of what to do to help her husband, she suddenly felt it was time to move into action. She stood up and spoke words that surprised herself, as well as her children.

"O.K. girls, you stay here and tend to the phone. I'm going next door to see if I can borrow the Carson's cellular. Matt and I are going for a drive! Matt, you get the keys and open the garage door. Start the car and warm it up. You'll do the driving and I'll be the navigator. I know that territory as well as you do. Your dad and I have driven it enough that I can get around that area blindfolded!"

Matt stood there a moment in total and joyful shock at hearing his mother sound so sergeant-like. He then wheeled around on his heels and walked quickly to the key rack mounted next to the refrigerator. He felt a closeness to his mother in that moment that can only be generated by crisis.

Within five minutes, Evelyn returned with the Carson's fully charged cellular in her hand and went to her bedroom to get an item that she hesitated to carry. On her way to the garage to join her son, she stopped in the kitchen and said to her two girls, "You two are in charge here. Keep the phone line open. Don't have long conversations with anyone. We'll be at this number." She handed her oldest daughter a piece of paper with the Carson's cell phone number on it, and kissed her on the cheek. "We'll be back soon!" Both girls stood side by side, and as Evelyn walked out the door, they looked at each other as if to ask, "Was that our mother?"

Evelyn climbed in the mini-van next to her son and said, "Matt, I have no idea what we're doing except we've just gotta help your dad. I know in my heart that he needs us. And, I brought this along." Evelyn held up a spray can of mace that Joe had insisted she keep in the house for self defense. "Your dad feels more comfortable when I keep this handy. I keep it in the bedroom...in case he gets out of hand." Evelyn smiled sheepishly as she realized she was offering humor that was probably, hopefully, beyond Matt's years. She was thankful that he didn't laugh.

Evelyn continued, "I hope this thing isn't too old to use. It says here on the side, *stream reaches eight to ten feet.* Wouldn't it be awful to get that close to those two guys your daddy met today?"

As Matt pulled out of the garage, he replied, "Sure would, Mom! And if we do, I brought this." Matt reached into his windbreaker pocket and presented his small hunting knife to Evelyn. She looked at the knife, then looked at Matthew. "Well, what are we gonna do with these weapons, son? I suppose I can make them cry...and you can trim their nails. I'm sure *Rambo* would be impressed!" As Evelyn pushed the "close" button on her garage remote mounted above the window visor and looked back to make sure the door was going down, she heard Matthew quietly, but nervously, chuckle.

As the mother and son drove away and headed toward the Gleason farm, Trooper Wilson crept slowly between the fences that lined Mill Creek Road. While he was formulating a plan of action in the event that he encountered the two suspects, he looked ahead in the distance and saw a red pick-up truck coming his way at a rate of speed that was far too excessive for the type of road they were traveling.

CHAPTER NINETEEN

Jack hit the brakes when he saw the patrol car ahead of him and screamed over the noise of the open cab. "We've got problems, Shelby! We're gonna have to turn around and make a run for it!"

Shelby challenged the idea. "Hey, let's try going on by that cop. He don't know who we are. Just be calm and slide on by him!"

"It's probably worth a try," Jack answered. "Just keep the kid quiet, whatever you do!"

Thirty seconds later the patrol car and L.D.'s pick-up were nearly nose to nose. Wilson's heart pounded in his chest with excitement as he realized he was face to face with the two men that the city of Grandville desperately wanted to see behind bars. He could see a pair of heads, but he wondered where the third person was. He assumed Stan was somewhere in the truck and determined to proceed with extreme caution on the boy's behalf.

Wilson pulled to the side of the narrow lane, as most people did on Mill Creek Road when they met another vehicle. And, in a friendly sort of way, he put his arm out the window and waved the pick-up to come on by.

"Jack, he thinks we're locals," Shelby loudly whispered with his face straight ahead and his eyes turned to see the policeman. "Go on by and wave a hardy thank you, and let's get out of here. We can fool this guy! Just keep your gun handy in case somethin' goes wrong."

Jack started to slip on by the patrol car. He slowed to avoid appearing too anxious to pass, and when the vehicles were hood to hood, Wilson leaned his head out to speak to the strangers. Jack didn't want to do it, but he decided it would be best to oblige the officer, and brought the pick-up to a stop. The two vehicles sat side by side, window to window.

Wilson called on all of his training as a lawman and calmly addressed the driver of the truck. "Howdy, fellows. What's happenin' today?"

"Not much, officer. What brings you to these parts?"

As he looked from bumper to bumper of the truck, Wilson responded, "Just came out to give Mr. Gleason a visit. Say, what happened to your truck?" Wilson quickly thought of a cover for the question he had just asked to see how the driver would respond. "Did that storm that hit us the other night do that damage?" Wilson knew that Giles county hadn't had a serious storm in nearly a month.

"Yes, sir!" Jack was relieved that the cop had given him a way to explain the missing windshields. "That was one whale of a storm. Took a tree out, and took our windows with it!"

Wilson was amazed at how calm and collected the suspect seemed. He looked around Jack and saw that the passenger wasn't showing quite the same amount of composure. In an effort to further convince the two that he was not aware of their identity, and to protect the young boy who, he assumed, was most likely in the floor board of the truck, he asked, "Are you the Johnson brothers that live over off of Highway 12? You sure do favor Richard." Wilson pulled a name out of his memory from a time when he had lived on the other side of the state.

Jack was growing a little weary of the questions that were holding him back. Still, he felt it necessary to accommodate the officer. "Is it that obvious? He's our uncle."

Wilson saw the passenger press something down with his arms and hold them there. He assumed he had a hand over the boy's mouth and decided it would be best to end the conversation, calmly drive away, then call central on his radio. "Well, I guess you'll be gettin' those windows fixed. Otherwise, you'll be eatin' a lot of bugs!"

As Wilson was speaking, he looked in his rear view mirror and saw a white, Chevy Blazer approaching, and it triggered the memory of Carla's call about the vehicle spotted at the nearby bridge the previous evening. Before he pressed his accelerator, he offered one more statement to the pair he wished he could have been hand cuffing at the moment. "Hey, you all be careful. There's two men on the run from the law somewhere in the area. They're armed and dangerous. You haven't seen anybody like that, have you?"

"Oh...no, sir. But, if we do, we'll give you a call right away." Jack smiled with an expression that made Wilson's back fill with fear induced chill bumps. It was the type of grin he always assumed the devil would have worn.

Jack and Shelby were so rattled and preoccupied with getting by the cop that neither of them noticed the white vehicle that was approaching. Not wanting to risk even one more pair of eyes being able to identify him, Jack looked sharply to his right in order to hide his face as he drove by the Blazer. Earl was so nervous about connecting with the officer, the sight of the damaged pick-up didn't register in his mind. As a result, the two acquaintances managed to pass without noticing one another.

When the truck was less than twenty yards behind him, Wilson reached for his radio mic and pressed the button. He noticed his hands were shaking. "Car 5, to central. Carla, do you copy?"

"10-4, car 5. Go ahead."

"Do you have help on the way? I just spent five minutes with the suspects. I know they have the boy. I couldn't justify attempting a capture. The kid would've gotten hurt."

"There is a unit moving your way at this moment. They should be real close to you right now."

Wilson reported, "I've got a white Chevy Blazer behind me here on Mill Creek Road. That rings a bell!"

Suddenly, another transmission broke into the conversation with Carla. "Wilson, do you copy?"

"This is Wilson. Go ahead!"

"This is Jackson. We're five minutes from the Gleason place, rollin' at a good pace. What's your 20?"

"I'm west of the Gleason farm. I just encountered the suspects and they're headed your way. Don't turn your lights on. They've got the boy. We've gotta do what we can to get him back unharmed!"

"10-4, Wilson. We're alerted to the situation!" Jackson turned off his flashing, blue lights.

Jack was rolling at about 50 miles per hour as he drove by the Gleason residence and disappeared over the rise in the road. Shelby held his left arm, and his moans of throbbing pain were unheard above the noisy ride. Stan's cheek was wet with tears as he fought to maintain an attitude of bravery. It wasn't coming easy for him.

When Wilson looked in his rear view mirror and saw that the red pick-up was out of his sight behind him, he made a quick turn into a grassy area to change directions. Before Earl could make the same turn, Wilson drove by and gave him, and the Blazer, a fleeting glance.

Well beyond the Gleason driveway, Jack suddenly hit the brakes and started sliding side to side. Shelby looked up and saw the second patrol car coming toward them. "They're here, man. They know we're in the area. That cop back there knew who we were all along! Turn around, Jack!"

Jack shoved the gear shift into reverse and moved backwards, breaking the small trees that edged the road. Then he dropped the shift into drive and spun out as he sped back toward Wilson's car. As soon as he regained control of the pick-up, he saw Wilson's unit coming his way.

"I've got 'em in sight, Jackson!" Wilson radioed, as he felt for his weapon.

"You gotta let 'em go on by. Think about the kid!"

When Jack met Wilson's patrol car again on the road, he made no attempt to slow down. He rolled the truck up onto the short bank on the right side of the road, tore through the barbed wire fence, and into the field at the road's edge. As Jack went around Wilson's car, he saw the white Blazer that followed. As the two passed one another, Jack got a glimpse of the familiar face behind the wheel of the Chevy. He grunted with disgust and briefly entertained the idea of going after the ex-in-law who had "stood him up" at the Currey River Bridge the night before. However, once he was beyond the two vehicles, Jack gave the steering wheel a left jerk, bounced back onto Mill Creek Road, poured the gas to the engine, and sped off to a hopeful escape. By then, Earl realized who was in the beat up but familiar truck, which the officer was so intent on stopping. Without thinking twice about it, he decided to join in the pursuit.

Unaware of the chase that had developed three and a half miles away, Joe stood motionless in the quiet of the roadside. The lower limb of his compound rested in the waist belt holster. As he held it upright with his right hand, he reached into his left pocket to retrieve his watch to check the time. When he pulled the watch out, along with it came a portion of his pink tracking ribbon. He started to stuff it back into his pocket, but hesitated. He looked at the ribbon, and suddenly, he got an idea.

CHAPTER TWENTY

Jack was nearing the intersection of Six Mile Road when Shelby looked over at him and waved his arm to signal him to keep going. They flew on by the familiar road at about fifty five miles per hour.

"Don't kill us, Jack. I don't wanna die in the country!"

Jack had gone another mile and came to a ninety degree bend in the road. He barely slowed enough to negotiate the turn. As he slid sideways, he accelerated, then headed south on the road he had ended up on the night before in old man Scutter's truck. He was two minutes from Joe's position. Troopers Wilson and Jackson were not far behind, and closing fast.

L.D. knelt on the roadside and clutched the half loaded .357 in his fist. In the silence, he imagined the hand that had once held the weapon, and a hatred stirred in his heart. It made him nauseous to think about it. His thoughts then turned to Tricia and his head spun with sickening emotion. He assumed she had heard about Stan's dangerous predicament. He whispered to himself, "Let one of us be a weapon in your hands, God! Help us get my boy back!"

Bob was sitting low in Joe's truck with the cell phone to his ear. Suddenly a voice broke the silence. "Mr. Gleason, do you have a report for me? What do you see or hear?"

He sat up and looked around. "Just silence out here. The birds are singing...but they obviously don't know what's goin' on. Makes me envious."

"Yes, sir," the operator responded with a slight smile in her voice. "Please stay on line. I'll get back to you in a few minutes."

Joe ran from the middle of the road and back to the position he had been holding earlier. He picked up his bow, re-knocked his last arrow, and listened intently. Suddenly, a sound faded up in the distance. It was the familiar sound of gravel crunching under the weight of a heavy vehicle. The noise was accompanied by the low roar of an engine. His pulse began to double as he raised his bow and pointed it in a direction beyond his position, as if he expected the vehicle to come to a stop after it passed him.

Bill knew he was speeding excessively as he held tightly to the wheel of his Suburban. He reached across the big seat, grabbed his phone, and dialed Joe's cell number. He had memorized it three years earlier when the trio of friends had succumbed to technology and purchased their phones. Hearing the busy signal, Bill decided to call 911 and report his whereabouts.

"911 operator, can I assist you?"

"Yes, ma'am. This is Bill Foster, a friend of Joe Tanner. I wanted to report that I am on my way to the area of the Gleason farm in western Giles County to see if I can locate Mr. Tanner."

"Mr. Foster, I have Mr. Gleason on line with me. Would you like to relay a message to him, sir?"

"Please tell Bob that I am on my way. I should be in the area in about 15 or 20 minutes. Can you ask him to tell me where he is?"

The operator requested Bill to hold, and a few moments later, she returned. "Mr. Foster, Bob Gleason said that he and L.D. Hill are on Six Mile Road half way between Mill Creek and Highway 12. He said you'd know where that is."

"Yes, ma'am, I do. Tell him I'll join him there as quick as I can."

Bill ended the conversation and quickly pressed his "end" button to avoid the possibility of receiving instructions from the operator to stay away from the area. He was bent on helping his friends. As he continued down Highway 12 to the Mill Creek turn off, Bob called out to L.D. through the open window of Joe's truck. "Hey, L.D., come up here!"

L.D. looked up and down the road and saw that it was clear. He walked to Joe's truck and Bob announced the good news that they would soon be joined by a familiar face. At that very moment, Wilson sped by the Six Mile Road intersection and headed toward the sharp turn that Jack had successfully, but barely, managed.

Evelyn looked anxiously out the front window of the mini-van as she and her son passed the sign that marked the west edge of the town of Grandville. "Matt, I know you never dreamed you'd hear me say this, but could you drive a little faster? You're not 'Driving Miss Daisy' today!"

"Wow, mom, those really are strange words... coming from you," Matt responded, as he pressed the accelerator.

As they drove toward Mill Creek Road, Evelyn attempted to relieve the tension of the situation by offering her son a conversational distraction.

"Matt, do you like the way I cook?"

"Yes, ma'am. I sure do. I like it a lot. But...there is one thing I'll have to admit. I do like a good dose of grease every once in a while. Since you started cooking for dad's heart, I suspect we're all gonna live to be 200 years old. But don't get me wrong, I know it's best for us!"

"I miss the fat grams, too," Evelyn agreed, " but you know I have to help your dad out with his diet."

"I know, mom, but if I have a 'grease fix' I need to feed, I know where to get it."

Evelyn looked at Matt in shock. "And where would that be?"

"Over at Jim's market. They sell these corn dogs on a stick, and there's enough fat in one of those belly bombs to last me about a month!"

"Do you actually do that, son?" Evelyn's voice revealed her surprise.

"I've been known to do it on occasion," Matt admitted, then looked at his mother to see if her expression revealed any evidence of having been offended. "Are you hurt?" .

"No... Are you?"

As Matthew laughed at his mama's quick wit, Evelyn conceded with a motherly sigh, "I suppose I should be happy that at least it's not drugs you're going for." It was a satisfying feeling to realize that she and her young son were able to carry on a conversation. Then, the sobering reality of the situation they were driving towards returned, as she thought of how much she hoped Tricia would be able to talk again with Stan.

Wilson's mind swarmed with strategy as he drove toward the sharp turn that was only fifty yards ahead. He had allowed himself the mistake of being distracted, and when he finally saw the 90 degree turn, it was too late. He dropped the radio microphone he was holding in his right hand and grabbed the wheel. His front tires bounced through the ditch and the front of the car went airborne. The mid-frame of the patrol car landed on the three foot embankment, causing the rear of the car to bounce wildly upwards, and then it landed hard on the ground. Wilson fought to make a left turn. His speed quickly sent him sideways in the field he had entered, and the right front and rear tires dug into the soft soil. Suddenly the left side of the vehicle raised completely off the ground, and he knew he was about to turn over. As the black dirt and soybean plants flew by his right window, Wilson put his hands on the roof of the car. Within seconds, he was hanging upside down, held in place only by his seat belt. He quickly assessed his health and decided that he was virtually unharmed, except for the throbbing of his left thumb he had jammed on the roof as the car flipped.

He had the presence of mind to turn off his motor, and when he did, he could hear another engine still running nearby. After wrestling with the seat belt, it unlatched, and Wilson fell to the roof of the car. He shot a quick glance at the feet that he could see running toward his wrecked unit. He looked passed the feet of the approaching stranger, saw the familiar, white Blazer parked at the edge of the road, and assumed the person was an accomplice to the suspects. He quickly grabbed his pistol, crawled half way out of the overturned car, and looked up. "Stop or I'll shoot!"

Earl stopped in his tracks. "It's O.K. officer, I'm on your side. I just want to help!"

As Wilson passed on through the open window and crawled out onto the ground, he looked beyond the Blazer and saw Jackson's car was pulling up to the scene. Then he looked back at Earl. "Who are you, Mister?"

"My name is Earl Potter and I'm a relative...ex-relative...to one of those guys you are chasing. It's a long story, but believe me, I want to get these guys as much as you do!"

Jackson ran up to the two men standing by Wilson's ruined unit, and looked at his disheveled fellow trooper. "Are you O.K., man?"

"I'll be fine. Those two guys are just in front of us. We've gotta go!"

Wilson and Jackson started to run to the remaining patrol car to continue their pursuit of the suspects, when Earl interrupted. "Officers, I live around here, and one of those guys is my former brother-in-law from Chicago. He called me last night and wanted me to help them get out of the county. I hate to admit it, but I started to help them out. Something went wrong, and to be honest, I'm glad it did. I never did connect with them. I'll explain it to you later if you'd like. Is there anything I can do to help you get them in custody?"

Jackson looked at Wilson, who was quite rattled by the exciting ride he had just taken. "What do you think, Wilson? Do we need this man's help?"

As he brushed the dirt off his pants, Wilson gave Earl some instructions. "We'd be grateful if you'd go back by Bob Gleason's farm and on to the end of Mill Creek. If you see any patrol cars on the way, wave them down and give them our location. If you get to Highway 12 and haven't seen any other units, wait there a while and then go on over to the Currey River Bridge and wait there. Do you have a cell phone?"

"No, sir. I'm sorry, I sure don't." Even without the ability to stay in contact with them, Earl enjoyed the good feeling in his heart in knowing that he was actually being asked to assist the law.

At the same moment that Wilson had begun his untimely ride in the soybeans, Jack was slowing the truck down. Shelby looked up with a puzzled expression on his face. "Why are we stopping, Jack? I think we've lost 'em. This is not a good time to stop!"

Jack leaned forward and wiped his eyes with the back of his hand. "What on earth is that up ahead?" He was referring to the twenty feet of pink ribbon that mysteriously hovered above the road about five feet high and parallel to the ground. He was too far away from it to see the ten feet of thin string Joe had attached to each end and tied to a tree on one side of the road and a fence post on the other. It blended so well into the background, it gave Jack the illusion that the hot pink ribbon was levitating by itself. Hanging from it, exactly in the middle of the road, was a five inch square of white paper. Shelby gazed at the sight. "Man, that's weird, Jack! Is the road closed?"

"It couldn't be. We were just through here last night. I know where we are now! Right back there is where we finally came out of those stupid fields by the river and got on this gravel road, remember? I'm tellin' you, we were here just last night, and it was open all the way to the pavement. This will take us back to the bridge! But first, let me see what this is hangin' across the road."

Jack slowly pulled the truck to within a half dozen feet of the pink obstruction to take a closer look. He leaned forward with his chest on the steering wheel, and with a surprised look on his face, he turned to Shelby. "Hey, are my eyes deceiving me, or does that paper have my name on it?"

Shelby quickly glanced at it. "It sure does. Maybe your buddy, Tony, put it there."

Jack opened his door to go check out the paper that was hanging from the ribbon. As he approached it, he saw the thin twine that held it in place, and threw his hands up in embarrassed disbelief. As he reached for the paper, Joe came to full draw about 35 yards behind them, undetected.

Jack held the paper sideways and saw that his name had been hand scribbled on it in large letters with black ink, and written over what appeared to be some type of official form. Under his name in smaller letters was written, "Please, turn the paper over." When he looked on the other side, his blood chilled as he read the words out loud. "I have you in my sights." It was signed...*Robin Hood!*

CHAPTER TWENTY-ONE

Jack quickly let go of the note that Joe had written on the back of his hunting license. He hastily looked around in all directions, and then, in an effort to make himself a hard target for the concealed archer, he crouched down and started darting back and forth in front of the truck. Just the thought of being run through by an arrow was much too painful to deal with.

Shelby was bewildered at the sight of his friend acting like a bug around a light bulb. "What are you doin' out there, Jack?"

"You better get low, Shelby, if you don't want another hole poked in you." Jack hurried as he came around the truck and nervously slid into the driver's seat. With his head just high enough to be able to see above the dash, he quickly put the truck in gear and started to drive away. Shelby couldn't help but shiver at the thought of hearing the snap of the bow limbs again.

Joe heard the click of the transmission, and before Jack could press the gas pedal, the last of his four arrows was in flight. His white pin was resting on the left rear tire when he released the string. The sharp field tip of the arrow, that was screaming at nearly 280 feet per second, found its mark. The shaft penetrated the rubber tire and was sticking out about ten inches, acting like a plug. However, when Jack rolled the truck forward, the arrow broke in the gravel, and the sudden, familiar, loud whooshing sound of a deflating tire caused Jack to come to an abrupt stop.

In the confusion of the moment, Jack hit the gas and the truck started to immediately fishtail left and right, then plunged into the ditch on the side of the road. The frame that hung lower than normal due to the flat tire caused the truck to lodge in the ditch, and Jack tried unsuccessfully to back it out. Realizing that they were stuck, and not wanting to encourage the nearby hunter to shoot another aluminum missile, Jack felt they had only one option. "Shelby, we've gotta run for it. I'm not gonna get this thing out of this ditch. You grab the kid and let's hit the woods. Just keep moving if you don't wanna get plugged again!"

Jack quickly opened his door and hit the ground running, thrashing into the cover of the brush that lined the road. He didn't bother to turn around as he tore through the thick woods and ran out of sight.

Shelby threw his door open, clutched Stan by the collar of his shirt, and slung the young boy onto the road. Stan managed to land on his feet, and as he was fighting for balance to stay upright, Shelby swung himself around to follow him out of the truck. As he attempted to exit the vehicle, the six feet of thin green line stretched tight and caused him to stumble face down onto the rocky surface of the road. Still attached to the seat in the cab by one leg, and falling to the ground, Shelby lost his grip on Stan, and the young man took off running around the rear of his dad's pick up. As he rounded the tailgate, he gasped when he saw another person running toward him. Stan was relieved and grateful when he recognized the painted face of Joe Tanner.

"He's tied to the truck, Mr. Tanner!" Stan excitedly announced. "He doesn't have a gun, but the other guy does!"

At that news, Joe quickly checked to make sure Jack was not returning and stepped around the truck to within five feet of Shelby, who was grabbing for the small rope that held him captive. Without hesitating, Joe came to full draw again, even though his quiver was empty. With the sun behind him, and knowing that Shelby would have to look up into the light, Joe guessed that his captive would not be able to tell that the bow rest did not have an arrow in it.

Joe stared across his bowstring at the struggling suspect. "Sit right where you are, mister, or I'll pin you to the ground!"

Shelby looked up at Joe, who was standing ominously over him with the bow pointed right at his face. The feeling of looking down the rest of the vicious looking contraption motivated him to abandon his attempt to escape. He put his head back on the gravel, and put his wounded arms out to his side.

As Joe moved around Shelby to insure that his captive would not be able to detect that his bow was not loaded, he heard another vehicle approaching the scene. "Whoever it is, Stan, wave them down!"

"Mr. Tanner, it's the police!"

Shelby groaned at the news, and Joe said a familiar word, as he looked beyond Stan at the dark, gray patrol car. "YES!"

Jackson stopped his vehicle at the rear of the red pick-up that was stalled in the road. Both troopers exited and pulled their weapons out of their holsters.

"Wilson, you're a sight for sore eyes!" Joe said, while relaxing the tension on his bow. "Man, I didn't know if I could've kept this thing at full draw for another minute." Joe looked down at Shelby, caught his eye, and mockingly announced, "Even though it *was empty!*" When Shelby saw there was no arrow on the string, he grabbed a handful of gravel and threw it at the truck in defeated disgust, then moaned as he clutched his arm.

Wilson pointed his gun at Shelby. "Who you got there, Mr. Tanner?"

As he held the bow down at his side, Joe responded, "This is the yahoo that emptied his weapon at me this morning. It's a wonder that I'm still alive. I can prove he's the one that shot at me. There's a hole under each of his arms. I personally put them there. The other guy took off up through the woods!" Joe looked anxiously up the hillside towards his unsuspecting friends, and as if entering into the mental zone where no excuse for defeat is accepted, he added softly and slowly, "...and it's not too far up the hill to where L.D. and Bob are waiting." He knew in his heart that he had to go to them.

Jackson walked back to his patrol car, radioed to central, and reported the turn of events. Trooper Wilson replaced his pistol in his holster, knelt over Shelby, and helped him sit up. He then took his handcuffs and proceeded to secure his prisoner's arms behind his back. As he did, he looked at the nylon string that held Shelby in place by the shoelace. "Who's idea was this?"

"That was mine," Stan said proudly. "Would you like for me to cut him free for you? I have a knife."

"If you don't mind, little buddy, I'd appreciate it," Wilson responded, and continued his praise of Stan's clever trap that had snared Shelby. "Looks like you caught yourself a big fish today!"

"Yes, sir. I reckon so."

Shelby glared at Stan as the young man proudly walked over and pulled the knife out of his pocket, then ran the blade through the stringer.

Stan was watching with widened eyes as the policeman man-handled Shelby toward the patrol car. Wilson grinned when he saw the boy's amazed expression. "I don't think we'll use the catch and release method on this big fish. What do you think, little buddy?"

Stan answered the trooper with a smile in his voice. "No, sir, we won't!"

With Shelby confined securely in the caged back seat, Jackson finished his communication with Carla and hung his microphone back in its clip. "Wilson, looks like there's another unit and a wrecker on the way. When they get here, we can send this guy on to jail and let them take the boy home to his family. Then we can join in the search for the other suspect. Also, there's another fellow on his way to this area by the name of Bill Foster." Jackson exited his patrol car and looked around for Joe to ask him if he knew Mr. Foster, and discovered the camo clad hunter was nowhere in sight.

"Where did Mr. Tanner go?" Jackson inquired.

Wilson looked in all directions and immediately presumed that Joe had gone after the other suspect. He was not aware that Joe felt so intensely responsible for L.D. and Bob's well being that, after placing his empty bow in the bed of the pick-up, and without telling anyone, he slipped off to get to his friends before Jack managed to do the same. He was also driven by the distraught look he remembered on L.D.'s face when Stan had earlier disappeared in his truck with Jack and Shelby. He was determined that L.D. would not have to wait one minute longer than necessary to hear about his son's return to safety.

"Well," Wilson said, with an understanding sigh, "At least he's dressed for the dangerous journey. May the Lord protect him...especially when Evelyn hears about this!"

As Joe cautiously hurried back up through the early October woods to his friends, he was being slapped in the face by low hanging branches. He stopped to rest and to carefully listen for any audible signs of Jack's presence on the hillside. Confident that the way was clear, he didn't hesitate to press on. He guessed that he was within seven to ten minutes of Bob and L.D., and he was certain he would come out on the road near his disabled truck. Little did Joe know that only a few minutes earlier, Jack had wandered up the hill across the very same path.

CHAPTER TWENTY-TWO

Only an hour and twenty minutes of daylight remained when Jack stumbled onto the edge of Six Mile Road. He was nearly hyperventilating as he looked up and down the lane to see if it was clear. He had not given a thought to Shelby and the kid. Instead, he was engrossed in self survival, and assumed that Shelby would fend for himself. As for Stan, he didn't care.

As he stood in the open space of the gravel road, he pulled out his .357 and checked the load. He mentally retraced the steps he and Shelby had taken that day and determined that he was back on the road where, earlier that morning, he had first encountered the man he resentfully referred to as *Robin Hood*. He recalled that as he and Shelby approached the truck that they had disabled, they were walking uphill. He decided that if he turned right on the road and headed downhill, he would eventually return to the bridge, and at least be reunited with the money stashed under it. As he began to walk south on Six Mile Road, he suddenly heard a vehicle approaching behind him. Not willing to take the risk that it was the police, Jack quickly jumped into the brushy edge of the road and hid himself. He was not aware that only 400 yards around the bend, the two men he had left behind in a mad rush just a little while earlier were standing by, waiting for Bill to arrive.

Bill was not sure how close he was to his friends and moved carefully along the road. As his vehicle rounded the turn, Jack saw that it was not a patrol car, but a large, dark green Suburban. He stood motionless, and was unseen, as it slowly rolled by. Once past him, Jack ran to the rear window and slapped it twice with his hand.

The brake lights came on, and Bill came to a stop.

Assuming it was L.D. or one of his other buddies, Bill lowered his window and looked over his left shoulder. Suddenly, without expecting it, he was staring down the loaded barrel of a huge pistol.

"Don't move, mister," Jack demanded, as he reached for the back door behind Bill.

"All...right," Bill responded nervously. "I thought there were two of you?"

Jack was livid. "Just keep your mouth shut. You talk when I tell you to talk." Jack slid into the rear seat while holding the gun to Bill's head.

"I don't know where my partner is, and frankly, I don't care. But you're gonna help me get out of here. You're gonna take me down to the big bridge at the bottom of this hill, and then you're gonna take me out of this area completely!"

Bill didn't dare make any fast moves, or say a word. The silhouette of the silver Smith & Wesson at his ear was motivation enough to follow the man's orders.

"Are you familiar with these parts?" Jack inquired.

"Yes, I am. You're about two miles from the main road and the bridge you're talkin' about. Once we get to the main road, the bridge is to the right. Listen, why don't you just take my truck and leave me here? This baby will take you anywhere you wanna go."

Jack was surprised his captive didn't already know the answer to the question. "Cause things have gotten too messy, and I need you for insurance. Now, shut up and drive!"

Bill slowly continued, and within less than a quarter of a mile, he looked ahead and saw a familiar white and blue pick-up truck sitting on the left side of the road. Jack remembered the truck as well, and he firmly pressed the end of his pistol into Bill's neck. "Punch it, speed up, go on around that pick-up, and don't slow down!"

A few minutes earlier, L.D. had gone to the rear of the truck to wait for Bill's arrival and was sitting on the tailgate, staring at Joe's 10 pointer and praying about the danger Stan was facing. Suddenly, he and Bob heard the roar of the engine as Bill rounded the turn, and they were excited to see that their friend had arrived. L.D. laid the pistol on the tailgate, assuming it wouldn't be necessary to have it in hand, and walked to the middle of the road to greet his buddy. As Bill grew closer, Bob noticed he was speeding up. "L.D., I don't think he's gonna stop!"

Jack screamed in Bill's ear. "Run over him!"

"I can't do that, mister!" Bill boldly defied the order and swerved to miss his friend. The quick movement of the large vehicle caused the Suburban to lose traction and slide in the gravel, and it ended up sitting sideways in the road about twenty yards beyond where L.D. stood, frozen in confusion.

Bob put the phone down on the front seat, exited Joe's truck, and was about to join L.D. when suddenly, the right rear door of the Suburban flew open. Jack decided that he had no other choice than to corral the trio and use them all as hostages. He quickly started barking orders, and the two surprised men were motivated to submission by the sight of the large weapon Jack pointed at their chests. L.D. looked longingly toward Joe's truck, regretting that he had left his only defense laying on the tailgate.

"You, old man, get in the front seat." Jack then looked at L.D. with a rage in his eyes that was sickening. "You're the kid's dad aren't you? Well you'll be happy to know that he's still in good hands with my buddy. Now get in the back and scoot over...and stay on your side."

Jack climbed in, put the gun to Bill's neck once again, and demanded, "Now...drive! And, none of you talk unless I ask you to!"

As Bill was moving in reverse to point his vehicle downhill and drive away, Joe came near the edge of Six Mile Road. It had taken him longer to get there than he wanted, but he was pleased that he had returned within sight of his truck. However, he was greeted with two surprises. One, he recognized Bill's green Suburban that was moving to his right. He noticed that there were four figures inside. When he saw the familiar silhouette of Jack, holding the pistol to the back of Bill's head, he immediately knew that L.D., Bob, and Bill had been commandeered by the gunman. Joe felt helpless as they sped off down the hill.

Wanting to avoid gunfire inside the vehicle, Joe stood motionless as the large truck passed him within twenty yards. His camo allowed him to go undetected, and as soon as Bill had gone around the bend, he walked forward to get to the edge of the road. That's when he discovered his second surprise.

As he stepped through the tall Johnson grass, he tripped over what he thought was a fallen limb. However, when he looked down to maneuver over it, he found an old friend. It was his compound bow and attached quiver full of arrows. After drawing it back and looking it over, he decided it was amazingly unharmed, and still in good working order. He whispered to himself as he looked down the road toward the Suburban that had gone out of sight, "Thank God. At least I'm armed again!"

Matthew gave his turn signal a downward push, guided the minivan onto Mill Creek Road, and proceeded toward the Gleason Farm. Evelyn dug into her purse, found the Carson's cell phone, and dialed 911.

"911 operator. How can I assist you?"

"This is Evelyn Tanner. I am inquiring about the status of my husband, Joe Tanner. Lance Wilson instructed me to check with you if I needed information."

"Yes, ma'am, Trooper Wilson informed us that your husband is returning to his vehicle at this moment. Also, you will be glad to know that Stan Hill is in safe hands."

Evelyn looked up and sighed with relief, then smiled as she looked at Matthew. He knew she had favorable news. She continued to listen as the operator added, "It was reported that your husband's truck is on Six Mile Road. Do you know where it is, Mrs. Tanner?"

"Yes, we know. My son and I are going there right now. Thank you for your help."

Evelyn ended the call and looked at her son with a wide smile. "Matt, I have good news and... I have good news! One, Stan is safe. Hallelujah! The other good news is, your dad should be at his truck on Six Mile Road. Let's get there as quick as we can with the least amount of damage as possible to my van."

In the joy of the moment, Matthew looked at his mother and noticed the tears of joy that quietly filled her eyes and accompanied her relieved countenance.

Joe hurriedly ran across the road to his truck and found the driver's door still opened. He picked up the phone and looked at the small window on its face, and the words *in use* were illuminated. He quickly put the phone to his ear. "Hello!"

The 911 operator responded, "Yes, Mr. Gleason, I'm still with you."

"Ma'am, this is Joe Tanner!"

"I'm sorry, I thought I was on line with Bob Gleason...Mr. Tannner? How did you get on line with me?"

"I returned to my truck and found that Mr. Gleason, L.D. Hill, and Bill Foster are all three hostages now. As I was arriving, they were driving away and Mr. Foster seemed to be at the mercy of the suspect who is still at large. He's still armed, too! Please let Trooper Wilson know about this, and tell him they were headed toward Highway 12. As soon as he can, he should continue down the road he's on and it'll dump him onto another road, which will lead him to Highway 12."

"I will relay that message right away to Trooper Wilson and... Mr. Tanner, I need to tell you that I just spoke with your wife. She and your son are on their way to your location. They should be there any moment. I spoke with her less than five minutes ago."

"Oh! Thank you, ma'am. I'm gonna go off line now and wait for them! Thank you so much!"

Joe's emotions swirled with joy and despair as he thought of seeing Evelyn and Matthew again, and then realized what misery his three friends were feeling. He also thought of the roller coaster ride of emotions that Tricia would experience when first she heard the news of Stan's return to safety, and then, when the report of L.D.'s latest predicament reached her. He also knew that Donna would not be left out of the barrage of horrifying emotions when she learned of the criminal capture of her husband. In the stillness of the roadside, Joe looked up into the sky and worded a prayer. "We still need you down here, Father!"

CHAPTER TWENTY-THREE

Earl Potter felt that he had waited long enough at the intersection of Mill Creek and Highway 12. He decided to continue on, and when he reached the Currey River Bridge, he parked his Chevy Blazer at the east end, within sight of Six Mile Road. He remained there just as Trooper Jackson had instructed. As he sat with his window rolled down in the stillness of the river area, he was dealing with a mixture of regrets. He was not only sorry that he ever agreed to help Jack, he was also emotionally back peddling in regards to his decision to face the truth about his past. Earl still wanted desperately to maintain his anonymity in the community he had grown to enjoy, but he assumed his life was about to drastically change. He was tempted to drive away from the bridge he was visiting for the fifth time in less than twenty four hours. As he struggled with whether or not to simply hurry to his house, grab a few things, and forever leave his Giles County home behind, he saw a large, late model Suburban come to a sliding stop at the end of Six Mile Road.

As the dust boiled up behind the stopped vehicle, Earl put his hands on the ignition key, ready to start his engine. The unfamiliar vehicle turned right and accelerated as it rolled toward Earl. When the two vehicles were side by side, Jack looked out the window and got another momentary glimpse of the familiar face he had seen back on Mill Creek Road. He immediately screamed, "Stop the truck! Stop right here!"

Bill mashed the brake pedal and all of the men lunged forward. Jack held his gun tightly in one hand and shoved with the other. "Get out of the truck. Get out! Right now!"

Earl was puzzled at the sight in his rear view mirror. The people were suddenly exiting the vehicle that was just behind him. Also, he had not seen Jack in the back seat. As he watched the scene unfold, he assumed the men were authorities who had come to assist the Troopers in the pursuit of the bandits.

Jack was the last one to exit the Suburban and he waved his pistol frantically in all directions. Earl couldn't believe his eyes when he saw who the gunman was. He quickly started his motor, and before he could drop his Blazer in gear, Jack's gun barrel was in his face.

"Hello there, Tony!"

Bob and L.D. looked at one another, then looked at Bill. The three of them had never before heard Earl referred to as *Tony*. Their curiosity was not long entertained as they watched Jack grab Earl's door by the handle and forcefully swing it open. "I wanna see your hands, Mr. Manzana!" Earl put his hands into the air and sat motionless in the Blazer.

"Why don't you let these guys go, Jack, and I'll help you get out of here!" Again, the three friends were amazed. They wondered how Earl could have known the suspect's name. Each of them independently was hoping that their captor would agree with Earl, and that they would be set free to return to their families. But it was not to be.

"No way, Tony. We're all gonna get in your hot little Chevy, and you're gonna take me to a safer place. I'm gonna need the rest of this bunch for a shield if the guns go off!"

Jack walked over behind Bob, put his arm around his neck, and placed the gun at his temple. "If you don't want to see this old man's lights go out, then all of you, get in the Blazer!"

The group took their seats in the Blazer with Earl at the wheel, and Bob between him and Bill. Jack was in the rear seat again on the driver's side, and sat across from L.D. He pressed the power button for his window and when it was fully down he instructed Earl to move in reverse. As the Blazer rolled backwards, and Jack was next to the front of Bill's vehicle, he sharply said, "Stop!"

Earl obeyed, bringing the Blazer to a halt. In nearly one fluid motion, Jack put his pistol out the window, quickly fired two rounds into the radiator of the Suburban, then he put the barrel of the gun in L.D.'s ribs. The four men shook as the gun roared and the bright green fluid began pouring out of the vehicle. Bill couldn't believe what had just happened, but he was so stunned that he couldn't say a word.

Earl was totally mystified. "Man, why on earth did you have to do that? We could've taken that truck. It's newer, you know."

"Just because it felt good, Tony. And, to show these guys just how bummed I am for you not being at this bridge for me and Shelby last night...like you said you would! Anyway, there'll be plenty of room for just you and me in this thing...in a little while! I don't want to have to stop every ten minutes for gas!"

The curiosity got the best of Bob at that moment and he couldn't hold back the question any longer. "Do you guys know each other?"

Jack was extremely irritated at the inquiry, and he yelled loud enough that everyone's ears nearly bled at the sound of his voice. "Don't talk to me. Don't ask me questions. If I want you to know anything, I'll tell you!! Now drive." As Earl drove east, Jack's worried glance back at the bridge would have revealed one major source of his anger, had the captives around him known what he was leaving under it. As he tried to quickly memorize the structure and the surrounding area for future identification, Jack thought to himself, "I'll be back!"

When Wilson had heard the two gun blasts in the distance moments earlier, he reached for the microphone in Jackson's car and pressed the button.

"Carla, this is Wilson, do you have a copy?"

"Yes, come back."

"I just heard two gun shots. It sounded like they were about a mile away. Can you tell me when the other unit will be here? We need to send our captive back to town and go check out the gunfire. I have a feeling it involves the remaining suspect, as well as the crowd he has gathered in Bill Foster's truck that you reported a few minutes ago. We can't sit around here very much longer. Where is everybody?!"

Carla could tell that Wilson was perturbed at the lack of assistance, and she quickly answered, "One unit is coming out by the river road, another is on the way to your location, and a third unit is abandoning a roadblock on the east side of town. It will also be coming your way. Plus, we're requesting help from Starkton. We'll dispatch any units they send as quickly as possible. And by the way, there is another wrecker coming to tend to your unit."

Officer Randy Tibbs broke into the communication. "Wilson? Tibbs here. I just passed what I assume is Six Mile Road. My E.T.A. to your 20 is less than five minutes. Do you copy?"

"10-4, Tibbs. Please hurry up, but let me warn you, there's a sharp curve ahead of you in less than a mile. You'll find my unit there." Wilson was embarrassed to tell him the details. "If you don't take the curve carefully, you'll end up on top of it!" He then turned his call to central. "Carla, have you spoken with Mrs. Tanner since she entered the area?"

"Negative, Wilson. She was enroute the last time we communicated."

"Have you heard from Earl Potter?"

"Negative," Carla answered.

As Wilson anxiously watched for Tibbs to arrive, Trooper Jackson entertained Stan with an explanation of all the gadgets and tools of his trade that filled the car. The observant officer knew that the young fellow was worried about his dad. As he handed Stan his handcuffs to examine, Jackson speculated about Earl. "I wonder if Mr. Potter is on the up and up. I sure hope he didn't pull the wool over our eyes. He seemed sincere enough to me. How about you?"

Wilson pondered the question as he anxiously looked behind him. "I don't know, Jackson, but I'm with you. If he was fooling us, he did a good job. But if he's on the sly, why would he have chased us down and offered to help? Let's just hope he's on our side."

As Wilson was finishing his sentence, he saw a patrol car coming from behind, in the distance. Within moments, he and Jackson exited the car, greeted their partner, and handed the weary prisoner over to him. Stan was grateful to get to be the front seat guest of Trooper Tibbs, and he waved thankfully at Wilson and Jackson as the two officers departed and headed to the Currey River Bridge.

"Looks like you've had a pretty exciting day, young man," Tibbs said to Stan, as they climbed into his patrol car.

"Yes, sir. It's one I guess I'll remember for a long time. I sure hope my dad is O.K. Do you think he's all right?"

Tibbs saw the aching concern that Stan showed on his face, and attempted to offer the young man a bit of comfort. "Well, let's hope for the best. At least we'll see to it that his truck will make it back to town safe and sound. The wrecker should be here soon. We'll stay here 'till it does. As for the guy back there," Tibbs pointed at Shelby with his thumb, "he's not goin' anywhere...but to the big house."

As Stan wondered where the "big house" was that the officer spoke about, he politely smiled, looked out over the dash of the patrol car, and whispered a prayer for his captive father.

A few minutes later, Wilson and Jackson pulled onto Highway 12 and turned right. There, they discovered Bill's Suburban sitting at the end of the bridge, facing west.

"Man, looks like somebody ought to start a junkyard business out here. This must be Mr. Foster's truck. Somebody has shot this thing. The radiator has been leaking like a broken water main!"

Wilson looked across the bridge, then eastward down the highway. "I wonder where everybody is?...Jackson, do you remember what Mr. Potter said about one of the suspects being a relative of his? I have a hunch that he was sitting right here, just like we told him to be, when Mr. Foster's truck came off the hill, full of hostages. I would guess that the whole bunch is in that white Blazer. And, I have a feeling that empty radiator explains the two gunshots we heard a while ago. Let's put the bumper to this truck, get it off the road, and see if we can find them. I suggest we go west a little ways first. I can't imagine the suspect wanting to head back toward Grandville. He knows he's not welcome there."

The two troopers pushed the abandoned Suburban to the side of the road, radioed to central for another wrecker to be dispatched to the area, then cautiously headed west.

Joe had also heard the two shots. As he sat on the driver's side of his truck with the door opened and one foot on the ground, he worried about what the gunfire meant. He was intensely anxious to find out.

The quietness of his surroundings did not represent the chaos of the day he had been having. His body was tired and screaming for food, water, and rest. "Enough of this adventure," he whispered, "I need to take my 'ticker' home. But, I guess this day is a long way from over, cause I've gotta help my buddies...somehow. I need some wisdom." As he said the words to himself, he heard the crunching of gravel, and his heart raced with excitement when he saw his wife's plum colored mini-van come around the bend. With a wide smile on his face, Joe stepped out of the truck and into the middle of the road.

"Look, mom, there's dad!" Matt said, with a tone of deep relief.

"He sure looks worried and frazzled! I know he's bound to be hungry, too." Evelyn wished that the three of them could simply go home.

Matthew pressed the down button on the window as he carefully drove up to his dad. Joe leaned onto the top of the driver's door with his left hand, and gently put his right hand on Matthew's shoulder. He looked at his son, then sighed deeply as he looked across the van to his bride. "You'll never know how good it is to see you all again!"

Evelyn jumped out of the van, ran around to her husband, and gave him a grateful hug. "Are you O.K., sweetheart? You look worn out!" Tears of joy filled her eyes again as she lovingly patted Joe on his back, and felt the sweat soaked camo shirt splash under her hand.

Joe held Evelyn tightly, then looked at Matt, who was opening the door to join in the embrace. As they enjoyed a group hug, Joe spoke with a faltering voice. "I'm fine, but Bob, L.D. and Bill aren't doin' so well right now."

CHAPTER TWENTY-FOUR

Joe was tempted to sugarcoat the news about his three friends, and he struggled to hide the dread in his voice. "Well...we captured one of the suspects down the hill from where we are right now. He's in custody. Unfortunately, the other guy ran off, and he came back up the hill in this direction. I followed him up here, and a few minutes before you drove up, I arrived in time to see Bill drive away with Bob and L.D. in his Suburban. In the back seat was the second of the two culprits. The worst news is, I could see that he had a gun on Bill as they went by me. I'm not sure what to do now!"

Matthew inquired, "Which way did they go, dad?"

"They went downhill toward the Currey River Bridge."

"Well, let's follow them!"

Joe looked in the direction of the bridge for a long moment, then spoke with a tone of caution. "We've certainly got to help our friends, we have no choice. The fellow who has them hostage won't think twice about doin' what he has to do to avoid being captured, even if it means killing. His name, I found out, is Jack. Since he hasn't seen this van, I think we ought to go down there and see if we can find them. They must be somewhere on Highway 12. Just maybe we can get in sight of the Suburban."

Joe went to the cab of his truck, retrieved his cell phone, and handed it to Evelyn. "Honey, you operate this thing. Matt, you do the driving and I'll stay low in the back seat." Matthew's expression upon receiving his dad's instructions showed his gratitude that he was found trustworthy enough to help in the search.

"Before we leave," Joe announced, "there's a couple of things we need to take with us. I'll take my bow and anything else I can find in the truck that we might need. Evelyn, if you will, go to the back of the truck and get my hunting knife out of the orange rubber gloves."

Evelyn stepped to the tailgate and discovered the big buck that was decaying in the warmth of the evening. She sympathetically called out to her husband, "Sure is a nice deer, sweetheart. What a terrible shame for it to go to waste."

Joe looked through the rear window of his truck at his understanding wife and nodded in sad agreement, then continued his search of the cab for other useful items. As Evelyn looked for the gloves, her eyes fell on the .357 that L.D. left behind when Jack had surprised them a few minutes earlier. As she wrapped her hand around the cold, silver pistol and picked it up, she was surprised at how heavy it was. She glanced around the truck to see if Joe was looking, found him still preoccupied, and quietly slipped the gun into her coat pocket. After finding the knife wrapped in the gloves, still covered with dried deer blood, she returned to the van and climbed into the front passenger's seat. Unable to bear the thought of the danger that the gun represented, she decided not to tell Joe about it, and to reveal it only if it was absolutely necessary.

Jack took his .357 out of L.D.'s ribs and pushed the barrel into Earl's neck. With his eyes on the other occupants of the Blazer, he waved his sword of verbal intimidation. "You better cooperate, Tony. I know these guys don't want to see what a bullet can do to a mind. *A mind is a terrible thing to waste,* you know!"

"Take it easy, Jack," Earl argued. "You got a good situation here. You have a car full of hostages and you're the one holdin' the heat. Just don't get trigger happy on us. We'll get you out of this area. Mr. Gleason here knows the roads around these parts like the back of his hand. He can..."

Jack interrupted Earl's speech. "Hey, which one is Gleason?"

Bob held his hand up to identify himself, hoping to generate more conversation. He determined that talk was much healthier than gunfire. "I'm Bob Gleason. Earl and I are neighbors."

Jack paused for a moment. "Earl, huh? Nice name for a Chicago chump. What last name did you steal?"

"Potter. People around here know me as Earl Potter. Now ease up, Jack. Just be calm!"

Jack screamed again, and the sudden outburst reverberated in the small cab. "Don't tell me to be calm. I hate it when people tell me to be calm! I don't see that I have a reason to relax, *Earl!*" Jack said the name with mocking disgust. "I bet there's cops crawling all around here, and I don't want to be calm!"

"Jack, I know Mr. Gleason can lead us on some back roads, and get us over to the interstate."

Bob looked around Bill at Earl with a confident nod. "I can do it, Earl. There's a right turn just ahead and we can go back through the country to Highway 49, and that'll take us to the four-lane."

Jack put the revolver to the backside of Earl's head and looked at Bob. "You better be tellin' the truth, old man, or your neighbor will be movin' away for good!"

As Jack was delivering his deadly threat, Bob was beginning to mentally plot a course that would lead them back to Highway 12, the only major paved road in that part of Giles County. He knew there was no other way to the interstate within twenty miles, other than crossing the Currey River Bridge, but he discerned that Jack didn't know it, and prayed he would never find out. The elderly gentleman's goal was to avoid being in too remote a place with the crazed gunman and risking a bitter outcome.

As the Blazer turned right off the pavement and disappeared into the countryside, Matthew was coming to a halt at the end of Six

Mile Road. Evelyn looked to her right and saw the Foster Family Suburban sitting just off the highway at the end of the long bridge. "Look, isn't that Bill's 'Burban?"

Matthew pulled the mini-van close to the vehicle, and Joe quickly slid the van door open, then exited toward the truck. Matthew followed him, and the two walked by the pool of bright green anti-freeze on the road. "Dad, looks like their new 'Burban's got a bad leak."

Matthew opened the driver's door and popped the hood. Joe examined the radiator and announced, "That explains the two gunshots I didn't want to tell you about. I heard them a few minutes before you found me up on top of the hill. That jerk has put two rounds through the grill, but I'm relieved that apparently, only the truck is wounded."

Matthew looked around the area. "Well, they're not here. Where in the world did they go?"

Joe shook his head in bewilderment, walked to the back of the empty Suburban, and looked in the cargo area. "Ah-ha! Matt, look what I found!" Joe opened the rear gate and retrieved a crossbow with four bolts mounted in the quiver. "Bill got this thing for the coyotes and he let me shoot it about two weeks ago. It is an amazing apparatus, and it's fast too. Probably shoots these bolts at over 300 feet per second. I even remember how to load it. It shoots kind of like a rifle. You just look down the sights and squeeze the trigger. It has a safety, like a gun. We'll take this baby with us in case we need it!"

Joe wondered if his friends and their captor were either nearby on foot, or if one more unsuspecting passerby, in another vehicle, had fallen victim to Jack's desperate attempt to escape. As he climbed back into the mini-van and was about to direct Matthew to head west, one of the two cell phones chirped. Joe knew immediately it wasn't his. He was surprised to see Evelyn with another cellular, and as she was answering the call, a different phone came to life. Joe recognized the familiar tone, reached over the seat, and picked up his own cellular.

"Joe Tanner here."

"Mr. Tanner, this is the 911 operator. Where are you at this time?"

As he was explaining his whereabouts, Evelyn was answering her call. "This is Evelyn Tanner. Who's calling?"

"Evelyn, this is Tricia Hill. I guess you heard Stan is O.K. Praises be!"

"Yes, that was wonderful news," Evelyn was happy to respond.

"We're on our way toward the Gleason Farm. We're not quite to the Mill Creek turn off."

Evelyn asked, "Who's with you?"

"It's just me and Donna Foster."

"How did you get this number, Tricia?"

When Joe heard Tricia'a name, he looked at Evelyn with a questioned stare, then continued his conversation with the 911 operator.

Tricia was grateful to have Evelyn on the line. "I got the number from your industrious daughter, Bessie. She was kind enough to agree to watch all of our kids so Donna and I could join in the search for our husbands. When the station called and told us about the predicament they were in, there was no way we could sit around Grandville and not help out. Your girls are the best. Where are you?"

Evelyn dreaded to let Tricia know that only Joe was safe, and that he was with her. "Matthew and I are with Joe in our mini-van, sitting at the east end of the Currey River Bridge. Where exactly are you?"

"We're about eleven or twelve miles from you right now, and we're parked along the highway. We had to pull off in order to get a steady signal on the phone. We'll hurry up and join you there. Can you wait for us?"

"We'll wait. Just be careful!"

A few minutes before the two determined wives pulled back onto the highway, Jack had started complaining to Earl and Bob, "We've been out here in the 'boonies' much too long. When do you think we're gonna find the hard road again, old man?"

"Actually," Bob answered, "It's just in front of us." His well calculated twists and turns on the back roads had managed to sufficiently confuse the gunman, who had been preoccupied in watching the moves of all his captives. He had no idea that the hardtop road Earl was approaching was Highway 12, and that the bridge where Bill's wounded Suburban sat was only a dozen miles away. Bob was keenly aware that if Jack realized they had gone in a big circle and were headed back by his own house on Mill Creek Road, someone would surely get hurt. Though it was risky and dangerous, he was convinced that their welfare was best served by getting back to familiar ground. Believing that to be true, Bob gave further instructions. "Turn left here, and stay on this road for about a mile. Then turn right onto the next gravel road." As they turned back toward the Currey River, Bob said a desperate prayer in his heart. "God, we need a miracle here!" Realizing what Bob was up to, his three younger friends sat quietly in the Blazer and didn't say a word. They simply prayed as well.

Earl accelerated when they pulled back onto Highway 12, and he quickly reached the speed limit. As he sped around a turn, Bill suddenly stiff armed the dash, and loudly yelled, "Watch out, Earl!"

Everyone in the Blazer looked up to see a brownish colored, Honda station wagon pulling onto the highway. Earl hit the brakes and began to slide. When the tires squalled in refusal to rotate on the blacktop, Donna looked in her rear view mirror and saw the fast approaching vehicle. She knew it wasn't going to stop. "Hold on Tricia! We're about to get hit!!"

162

CHAPTER TWENTY-FIVE

As Earl's Blazer plowed into the rear of Donna's Honda, Bob joined Bill and put both of his hands on the dash in front of him to absorb the impact. L.D. was thrown forward. Earl held tightly to the wheel and managed to slow down enough before contact. Jack was nearly slammed to his knees, but recovered quickly, and maintained his guard on his hostages. They were all very fortunate that the collision was not as violent as it could have been. As the two vehicles sat crunched together in the highway, Bill was mentally processing the unbelievable sight in front of him. It was his wife's car! In the excitement of the chaos, he started to announce the identity of the driver, but decided to let it go unknown. L.D. had noticed the familiar wagon as well, and shot a quick glance at Bill. With expressions that only long time friends can learn to read, each of them silently agreed not to say a word.

Jack was re-situating himself in the back seat, and nervously shouted, "Back up, Earl, and let's get out of here. This thing is still running. Do it now!"

Earl immediately put his Blazer in reverse and backed away from the Honda. As the two vehicles separated, the shattered glass and plastic fell to the pavement. Jack leaned forward, reached around Earl's neck, and as he violently choked him, he pushed the hard barrel of the pistol into the back of his head.

"Watch what you're doin,' you idiot! I need for you to be alert! Now pull around the car, and let's go!"

L.D. spoke up. "Don't you think we ought to check on those ladies?"

"No way," Jack answered. "They're O.K. They can deal with it on their own. But somebody's gonna really get hurt if Earl don't drive!"

Earl put the Blazer into the forward gear and pulled into the oncoming lane to go around Donna's crumpled car. As they started to go by, Donna said, "Those idiots are gonna drive off! Quick, get a pen and something to write on, and get their plate number!"

Tricia looked into the tray between the two shaken but uninjured ladies and dug for a pen. As the Blazer rolled passed them, Donna looked out her window at the occupants of the soon to be "hit and run" vehicle and angrily said, "I wanna see the jerks who would do us this way."

Donna couldn't believe her eyes as she looked over her left shoulder at the faces that were about to go by. "Tricia! Look at this!"

With one hand still in the glove compartment, and her body stretched across Donna's lap in order to see inside the passing Blazer, Tricia saw the faces as they passed, and did a double take. "I do declare. Those 'idiots' just happen to be our husbands!"

As Earl maneuvered around the Honda, Bill was looking out his window. L.D. was staring out his as well, and when the two married couples passed and saw each other behind their walls of glass, they were in total shock. All four pair of eyes met, and all four jaws were wide open in surprise. Neither man could say a word, they just gawked in amazement. Bob looked around Bill and also got a fleeting glimpse of the two familiar ladies, and their worried faces disappeared as the Blazer headed west.

"Quick, Donna, give me the cell phone," Tricia requested with her hand out.

Donna handed the phone to her rattled friend, like a nurse putting a surgical tool into the hand of a doctor. Tricia punched the Carson's cell phone number and within five seconds heard the first ring.

Evelyn took the chirping phone off the dash of the van and pushed the green button. "Hello, this is Evelyn Tanner."

"Oh! Evelyn! This is Tricia. You're not gonna believe this, but our husbands, and Bob Gleason, are headed in your direction in a white Chevy Blazer. Donna says it looks familiar but we're not sure who's driving it. Whoever it was, they just plowed into the rear of Donna's car and drove away! Also, it appeared that there were five people crammed into the vehicle."

Evelyn could tell that Tricia was very nervous and relayed the news of the wreck to Joe. He asked for the cell phone. "Tricia, this is Joe. Let me suggest that you hang up, call 911, give your location, and let them know what has just taken place. Also, while you're on the line with the 911 operator, tell them to notify Trooper Wilson of your accident, and ask them to send him to the Currey River Bridge!"

"Will do," Tricia replied. "It's good to hear your voice again, Joe!"

"Thank you! Now, we just need to get you and Donna back with L.D. and Bill. Where are you right now, Tricia?"

"Well...we had just pulled back onto the highway when we got rear ended. We're about ten minutes from you! I think the car will run. We'll check it out."

Tricia ended her call and dialed 911. Evelyn announced to her son and husband that the Blazer full of men were headed their way. Joe pulled his cap off and ran his tired hands through his hair. "We've gotta come up with something quick. Our friends are hostages in that Blazer. We can't let it go by us!" As Joe ended his sentence, Matthew suddenly punched the accelerator of the van and headed east, away from the bridge.

"What on earth are you doing, son?" Joe quickly asked.

"Dad, I have an idea. It just came to me. If that guy thinks he's come up on an accident that is blocking the road, he'll have to stop.

He hasn't seen this van and won't suspect who it is. You could be out of sight in the cornfield with your bow, and if he gets out of the Blazer, you could...." Matthew couldn't bring himself to say it in front of his mother, but Evelyn finished the sentence for him.

"...Shoot him. That's what you meant to say, right Matt?"

"Yes, ma'am," Matthew said respectfully.

Evelyn looked out her window and raised her eyes skyward. "Lord, have mercy on us!"

Joe spoke up, and admitted, "It's a great idea, Matt. Do you have a good suggestion on how to pull this off?"

Matthew looked in his rear view mirror to make sure they were out of sight of the Suburban, checked both directions to be sure there was no other traffic, and then made a U-turn on the highway. As he pulled sideways in the road to block both lanes, he said, "I'll lay down on the pavement in front of the van, as if I've been hit, and Mom can act like she's tending to me. Dad, you can hide a row or two back in the cornfield." Matthew pointed to the tall, brown stalks of corn that lined the road just a few feet beyond the edge of Highway 12.

As Matthew was presenting the only idea that had come to any of the three, Evelyn was digging in the compartment below the radio in the middle of the dash. She took out three unused packs of fast food catsup and held them up. "These might help make it look real." She was just as surprised as her husband and son that she was quick to join in the charade.

Much to Evelyn's surprise, Matthew took his knife out of his pocket, opened the blade, and cut a two inch slit in his jeans on the outer side of his left thigh. Then he ripped a large opening in his pants. As he squeezed the bloated packages of catsup, he wiped the red paste on his exposed leg, and on his face and hands, then looked apologetically at his mother. "Sorry, mom. Gotta make it look real!"

He exited the van and hurried to the front bumper and laid face down on the hard road with his head and shoulders near the center of the van, and his legs protruding out to the side.

Joe grabbed the Carson's cell phone and handed it to Evelyn. "Call 911 and ask them to put you online with Trooper Wilson. When you get him, tell him where we are. If the Blazer comes into view, just act like you're really upset, and make it look good. Whatever you do, don't leave the line with Wilson. And Evelyn, I don't know what's gonna transpire here today, but I pray none of us gets hurt. The guy we're hoping to defeat won't want to stop here. You might ask 911 to call Donna and have her halt the traffic that's behind her, by parking sideways in the road, just in case Earl Potter is forced to turn around and head back east...I love you, Evelyn!" She returned a nervous but sincere smile.

Joe retrieved his bow and started to head toward the cornfield. As he backed out of the van, he glanced at the cargo area and noticed the crossbow. He suddenly got an idea that, at first, made his blood chill. But he believed it would be a necessary precaution. He quickly removed it, stepped on the loading bar and pulled the string back, locking it into the firing position. He then knocked a bolt onto the string and checked to see that the safety was on. He walked around to the front of the van, got on his hands and knees, and laid the contraption on the road, next to his son. "Matt, I'm gonna put you in charge of this thing. Use it if you have to, but make sure of what you're shooting. Remember, to aim it, you look down these sights, shove the safety off, and just pull the trigger. It'll recoil, but it won't hurt. Also, keep in mind that this thing will shoot level out to 35 or 40 yards. After that, the bolt will start to drop. Just remember to aim a little high if it's further than that."

Joe shoved the crossbow carefully up under the engine area and patted Matthew on the back. "Son, I always 'bless' the arrows I shoot when I'm in a *moment of truth*. If you have to pull the trigger on this thing, say a little prayer first...I love you, son!"

As Joe stood to his feet and brushed his hands off, he heard a firm, "I love you too, dad!"

Joe walked across the highway with his bow tucked up under his arm. As he eyed the spot he would hide in the autumn corn, Evelyn dialed 911. Earl held tightly to the steering wheel of his Blazer that shook in his hands as a result of the wreck, and Donna was slowly limping in her Honda toward the Currey River.

About a minute later, Wilson reached for the radio mic that hung from its bracket on Jackson's patrol car and pressed the button. "Carla, this is Wilson. Any news from Joe Tanner since you spoke with Mrs. Foster about the accident?"

"Yes!" she responded excitedly. "We just got a call from Evelyn Tanner. She reported that they are staging an accident just east of the bridge in order to slow down the oncoming vehicle belonging to Earl Potter. She said it contains the hostages, and the suspect is assumed to still be armed."

"Who are *they?*"

"Apparently, Mrs. Tanner and her son are blocking the road, and Mr. Tanner is with them."

"10-4, Carla. We're on our way. We're a few miles west of the bridge."

Wilson radioed for back up. "Tibbs, what's your 20?"

"We're with the wrecker that's hauling Mr. Hill's pick-up, and we're headed down Mill Creek Road. We're about two miles from Highway 12."

Wilson returned with new instructions for his fellow partner, "Tibbs, we need more professionals over here near the Currey River Bridge! I know you have the other suspect and Mr. Hill's son, but we need you to turn right on Highway 12 and join us. Keep your distance, but be ready to move in on foot at our call. I'll get back to you!"

"10-4, Wilson," Tibbs answered, and looked over at Stan. "You heard the man, little buddy. Check your safety belt! We're making a detour."

Carla broke in. "Central, to car 5."

"Car 5 here. Go ahead, central."

"I need to put you on line with Mrs. Tanner now. She needs to stay in contact with you."

"10-4, Carla. I'll hold for Mrs. Tanner."

Thirty seconds later, Wilson heard the anxious voice of Evelyn Tanner. "Wilson, thank God I've got you on line. I assume you know what's going on out here."

"Yes, ma'am. I do. We're moving as fast as we can to your location."

"That's good, Lance," Evelyn said, and added, " Joe suggested that Donna Foster block the road behind us. Can you call base and tell them to contact her to do it?"

"Yes, ma'am. I'll do it now. Don't hang up."

Wilson juggled his conversations, and Evelyn could hear him as he expertly relayed the messages to his communications base in Grandville. She looked around the van towards the east, and all was quiet...at the moment. Then Matthew spoke up from his prone position on the hard road. "Mom, if I have to use this crossbow, make sure you're out of the way!"

Evelyn leaned down, looked up under the van at the vicious looking weapon that waited within arm's reach of her son, and repeated a short, but desperate prayer. "Oh God, do have mercy on us!"

About eight miles east of the Tanner mini-van that sat in the middle of Highway 12, Earl was preparing to turn right onto Mill Creek as Bob had instructed. At the sight of the gravel road, Jack decided to take over the job of issuing directions. "Earl...I mean...Tony...just stay on the paved road. With the shape this hunk of junk is in, we don't need to take a ride on a washboard.

Bob challenged the decision in fear of what would happen if Jack saw the familiar bridge again. "I don't recommend that route, mister. That'll get you nothin' but trouble!"

Jack angrily slapped the elderly gentleman on the side of his head with his open hand. "Shut up, old man. I'm in charge here. Just keep goin' Earl, and step on it!" Bill started to retaliate, and the distinct sound that the hammer of a pistol makes when it's pulled back motivated him to change his mind. Everyone sat stunned and quiet as the Blazer lumbered toward the Currey River Bridge.

CHAPTER TWENTY-SIX

The highway was uncommonly quiet as Joe stepped backwards into the third row of the tall, mature corn, and then dropped to one knee. He removed his shooting tab from his shirt pocket and put it on his fingers. The mini-van was in view at about twenty yards away, but because of the corn stalks, he couldn't see too well beyond the front of the van. In the stillness, he could see Evelyn as she knelt and began her theatrics. The minutes that passed seemed like hours to the three family members.

"Evelyn, are you still with me?" Wilson asked.

"I'm still here, where are you?"

"We're about four miles off of Highway 12, on a side road. Once we get back to 12, we'll be about seven or eight miles from the bridge. Tell me what you see."

"Well, strangely enough I am kneeling over my son at this moment, who is laying halfway underneath the bumper of my mini-van!"

Wilson's voice revealed his intense curiosity for their actions. "WHAT?!"

"It's O.K., Lance. It's part of the act. If that Blazer comes our way, it'll have to stop. We've just staged an accident involving a pedestrian. Joe's over in the....."

Evelyn stopped in mid-sentence to listen. Joe's ears became radar-like as he and Evelyn simultaneously heard the distant low roar of a vehicle coming their way. Joe removed an arrow from his quiver, knocked it, and then wrapped the finger tab around the string.

"Speak to me, Evelyn," Wilson begged.

With the phone still to her ear, Evelyn peered over the hood of the van and looked through the clear windows. Her voice was shaking. "It's the Blazer! I can see it through my windshield!"

Wilson checked his seat belt and said to his partner, "Faster, Jackson, things are about to unravel on the other side of the bridge!...Evelyn, keep talkin' to me. What do you hear?"

"The vehicle is slowing down. He's slowing way down!"

"Just keep playin' your part, Evelyn. Make it look good."

"Well, that may not be so hard to do!"

As Earl slowed his Chevy, the voice behind him boomed in his ear, "Good grief, what now?" Jack's breath was putrid as he sighed deeply in disgust. "This is all I need!"

"Looks like someone's been run over," Earl said, as he crept slowly by the van.

Earl steered as far left as he could and saw the body on the road. Then he announced, "Oh! Man! Looks like it's a kid! And he's really bloody!"

L.D., Bill, and Bob were horrified at the sight, and their hearts sank in despair when they recognized Evelyn. They noticed the cell phone to her ear and it appeared that she was on the phone with an emergency crew. Each of them felt completely helpless and frustrated, knowing they were at the mercy of a madman.

Jack grabbed Earl by the neck with his left hand and dug his dirty fingernails into his skin. "Just go on around this mess. Don't you even think about stoppin' this time!"

"Hey, Jack! We've gotta help this lady, and that poor kid. Look at the blood on his face. At least you could let one of us out to help, and the rest of us will go on with you. You've got plenty of shields, you can spare one of us. Have a heart for once, Jack!"

The sight of the woman kneeling over the injured boy was gruesome enough that Jack decided to change his plan, for a moment. He instructed Earl to pull the Blazer well in front of the van, and then looked at Bill. "You, when we stop up ahead, get out and help that woman and the kid, and if you wanna see your friends alive again, you'll forget you ever saw me!"

Earl moved the Blazer at a snail's pace around the scene and stopped about forty-five yards in front of the van. As Bill got out of the Blazer, Joe slowly stood up, stepped forward to the edge of the corn, and came to full draw. Bill exited alone, and Joe whispered a wish to himself, as he put his 40 yard pin just above the left rear tire. "Get out of that Chevy, *Mr. Jack!* I dare you!"

Bob slid over to the far side of the Blazer and as he closed the door, Joe decided it was time to take action. Hoping to deflate the tire and force Jack out into the open, he let the string slide off his fingers and sent the arrow on its way. Sparks flew on the pavement as the arrow sailed underneath the Blazer, missing the tire by two inches, and skipping into the weeds on the other side of the road. He knew he had missed his mark.

As Joe was quickly removing another arrow from his quiver and placing it on the string, Matthew reached for the crossbow and pulled it to his shoulder. He shoved the safety off, and without hesitating, he put the tailgate of the Blazer in the sights. Just before he squeezed the trigger, he whispered, "God, bless this arrow!"

The eighteen inch bolt catapulted from the bow and rocketed toward the rear of Earl's vehicle. From Matthew's angle, the bolt traveled upwards, missed the tailgate, but pierced through the lower portion of the gas tank that was exposed below the bumper.

Joe was happily astonished when he heard the bolt connect with the Blazer, and said a firm, "YES!"

In the same moment, Matthew whispered, "YES!!"

Jack was stunned, however, by the sudden thump. "What the....was that?!"

"Must be somethin' caused by the wreck," Earl suggested.

Immediately, the strong smell of gasoline filled the vehicle and L.D. said in horror, "It's the gas tank! We've gotta get out of here! One spark and we'll all fry!"

Suddenly, Jack opened his door and backed out of the Blazer without taking his gun off of the passengers, and demanded that they remain inside. Earl was tempted to take the chance to drive away, but because of the fear of somehow igniting the gas, and also leaving Joe's family to deal with his unpredictable ex-in-law, he turned his motor off and sat still in the road.

Jack slammed the door shut, then stepped backwards away from the vehicle that was losing a gallon of fuel every thirty seconds. The road around him was wet with gasoline. He noted that the stream of fuel running down the pavement resembled a fuse to a bomb. He had not noticed, however, that Matthew had come to life, nor had his state of intense anger allowed him to see Joe in the cornfield. As a result, he didn't hesitate to pursue the deadly idea that came to him when he saw the "fuse" in the road. He simply seemed bent on destroying all the eyes that could identify him and send him back to prison.

With an expression that only the devil himself could construct on a man's face, Jack walked back about thirty yards from the tail-gate, and with one hand he reached into his pants pocket, pulled out a dollar bill, and put it between his teeth. He pressed it between his thumb and index finger and pulled it until it was fully extended. Then, with the same hand, he retrieved a cigarette lighter from his shirt pocket.

With Jack only about thirty yards from his position in the corn, Joe once again came to full draw. As Jack lit the dollar bill that he held in his teeth, Joe put his sights on the suspect's calf and released the razor tipped arrow. Jack screamed in pain as the broadhead ripped through his denim pants and sliced through his leg, severing

174

the muscle in his lower right calf. As he fell to the pavement, the pistol flew out of his hand and into the dirt and gravel at the edge of the road. The flaming dollar bill lilted downward like a falling leaf, and when it landed on the pavement, the gasoline ignited.

Earl was watching the scene unfold behind him and screamed. "Bail out!!"

Three doors flew open. L.D. helped Bob as the two of them ran and tumbled into the brush about twenty yards away. Evelyn and Matthew, along with Bill, took cover behind the van. Earl made the near fatal mistake of taking an extra second to grab his wallet under his seat, and at the last micro-second, he jumped away, just as his Chevy's gas tank exploded, sending an intense wall of heat in all directions. The sound of the blast was deafening.

As the white Blazer was turning into an ugly black heap of charred ruins, Jack held his bleeding calf in his hand, yet still was able to crawl toward his pistol. When he was about three feet from retrieving it, and potentially being able to take charge of the scene again, he suddenly saw a foot kick the gun another five feet down the road. When he turned to show fight with the person responsible, he was surprised to hear a female voice say, "Don't move, mister, or I'll put a hole in your other leg! And if that don't work, I'll drown you in this stuff!"

Joe couldn't believe his eyes as he quickly walked back onto the highway toward his wife. There was Evelyn, standing over Jack in a police like stance, holding a silver .357 in one hand, and a can of mace in the other. Both weapons were pointed directly at the humbled, and seriously wounded, suspect.

Jack moaned and turned over on his back, only to see a circle of people gathering around him like wolves at a fresh caribou carcass. Earl looked at the pitiful, bleeding, and scorched enemy that laid on the road. "Looks like you're surrounded, Jack!"

"Get me some help, Tony. I'm gonna bleed to death!"

176

Evelyn took her stare off Jack for a moment to look at Earl when he was addressed by his former name. As he removed his belt to use as a tourniquet, Earl gave Evelyn a glance that implied, "I'll explain later."

In the distance, as the sound of a siren grew louder, Earl taunted the captive. "Looks like you're gonna have all the help you'll ever need in just a few minutes, Jack!"

"You're goin' down with me on this one, Tony!"

"I don't know about that, Jack," Bob said as he took the belt from Earl and began to wrap it around Jack's leg. "Earl has an alibi. He was with me last night. When you and your buddy were terrorizing Grandville, Earl and me were havin' some of my famous fried chicken. I can vouch for him. And by the way, *Jack,* I'm really glad you took over as navigator back there." With his farm weathered hands, Bob cinched the belt painfully tight onto Jack's wounded leg.

As his former brother-in-law writhed in pain, Earl took the timely opportunity to dig through Jack's pockets and found a small black book. He tucked it safely into his shirt and said, "I don't think you'll need this anymore, Mr. Brewer." Jack offered little resistance to Earl's search and could only beg for medical assistance.

Joe stood by and nearly threw up at the thought of what he had done. As he surveyed the carnage, Matthew came up to his side, put his arm around his trembling father, and complimented him. "Good shot, dad!"

"Thanks! And, same to you, Matt. God has delivered us!" Joe hugged his young son tightly, then pointed to Evelyn. "Look at your mother. She sure is a sight, isn't she?"

Joe and Matthew smiled as they looked at Evelyn, still standing over Jack with the heavy .357 pointed at him. She was beginning to weaken under the realization of what had transpired. "I seriously doubt if I could even pull the hammer back on this thing." When Jack heard her confession, he rolled his eyes in self disgust.

L.D. stepped to Evelyn's side, and with a mixture of laughter and anger, he offered, "Would you like me to take over, Officer Tanner?"

"Please do, L.D.!" Evelyn answered, and handed the gun to the one person in the crowd who wanted most to have the suspects at gunpoint. When Joe saw the disdainful way that L.D. looked at Jack, he realized that his weary comrade was yet to hear the good news about his son. With an indescribable joy in his heart, Joe put his arm around his friend. "L.D., Stan is O.K. You're not gonna believe what your brave boy did to help us capture the other suspect. He sure does have a great story waiting to tell you. Your son is safe in the hands of the law!"

The relief in L.D.'s face was profoundly obvious as tears began to form in his eyes. He nearly collapsed as he motioned for Bill to come and relieve him from the pistol. He was grateful that the desire for revenge that raged in his heart was suddenly leaving.

Joe then addressed his wife as he put his arm around her to support her. "Where on earth did you get that gun, sweetheart?"

"I found it on the tailgate of your truck," Evelyn admitted.

"That's the pistol I found after you plugged the other guy earlier today, Joe. Remember?" L.D. said, as he wiped the tears from his eyes.

"Ah! Yes! I remember."

"By the way, Joe," L.D. added, "Nice shot!"

CHAPTER TWENTY-SEVEN

As the daylight began to fade into darkness, Trooper Jackson pulled his patrol car up to the smoldering scene, and along with Wilson, quickly exited. They both drew their weapons out of their holsters and held them upright as they approached the crowd that had gathered around the captured suspect.

"Step aside, folks. Thank you!" Wilson said, as he looked at the pool of blood on the pavement that had drained from Jack's wounded leg.

Bob looked proudly at Wilson. "Well, there's your other man. You won't be needin' those pistols, and you have the Tanners to thank for him layin' here on the road waitin' for you!"

Bill spoke up and complimented his elderly friend. "Oh sure, Bob. How about that little trip we took around the mulberry bush with this guy? That was a brilliant delay tactic! I was as lost as a goose back on some of those roads. I had no idea where we were!"

"Looks like we have a lot of folks to thank for this fellow being in custody," Trooper Wilson said, as he holstered his gun and prepared to cuff Jack's hands behind his back. "We need to get him to the hospital first. Then, he'll join his buddy for the ride back to Chicago. By the way," Wilson asked, "What kind of wound is this in his leg?"

Joe spoke up and apologetically said, "That's the result of a broadhead. Three razor blades clumped together at the end of an aluminum arrow!"

Trooper Jackson grimaced at Joe's description of the devastating implement and shook his head in pity when he imagined the pain that their prisoner was feeling. As they helped Jack up off the black-top, another car was pulling up behind Evelyn's van. Bill could see that it was Donna's crumpled Honda and he smiled as he handed the .357 to Bob, and ran toward his wife. Tricia got out and hurried to L.D.'s arms, and the two couples lovingly embraced.

Donna dug through her pants pockets, looking for tissue to wipe her eyes. "We could see the smoke a long way off and we just had to come and see what happened. Is everybody O.K., Bill?"

"Yep, except for the fellow that's handcuffed and bleedin' about the leg. They're takin' him to Giles Memorial. His buddy, I under-stand, has two new holes in his body, thanks to Joe's fine archery skills. Then there's Joe's truck sittin' up on the hill on Six Mile that won't start, L.D.'s truck has new air conditioning, I hear that Wilson's car is takin' a nap in the turn at Seven Mile, our 'Burban is bleedin' anti-freeze, our Honda is havin' serious back pains, Mr. Gleason's noggin got rattled, and Earl's Blazer lived up to its name. Other than that...everything's O.K."

As Bill continued his unique account of the evening's adventure, another patrol car was coming onto the scene and parked behind the Honda. Officer Tibbs opened the door for Stan, and he ran to L.D. and Tricia's arms. The three of them formed a happy bundle of fam-ily flesh at the road's edge. L.D.'s eyes once again started to swim in joyous tears as he said, "Hallelujah to the name of the Lord who has brought us together again!" Stan looked tenderly into his dad's watery eyes, and smiled. "Caught us a couple of big ones today, huh, dad?"

Officer Tibbs found Wilson who was wrapping first aid gauze around Jack's wound, and privately said, "Wilson, I just talked to central and I have some good news and bad news. The good news is they believe Phillip Simpson is gonna make it. The bad news is that your father-in-law, Mr. Scutter, was found nearly dead of a heart attack just a little while ago in his kitchen. First reports are that when they found him, he was mumbling something about having been attacked, and his truck stolen last night. He said he can identify the two men who beat him up at gunpoint. He's recovering at Memorial."

Wilson stopped his emergency medical attention and looked into Jack's eyes. His prisoner stared back with an empty look that was void of any sorrow.

Tibbs continued. "When the call came in about Mr. Scutter, my prisoner got really nervous. I guess adding car theft to his record was the straw that broke the criminal's back, cause he started to talk. He said it was this guy that master minded the whole affair, and he wants a separate ride back to Chicago. I took the liberty to bargain a little with him, and in exchange for the promise of isolation from his buddy, I found out about a couple of items these guys stashed that we'll need to retrieve. One, your father-in-law's old truck is below the bridge, and at the bottom of the river."

At that news, Wilson was tempted to "accidentally" close the door on Jack's leg, but he managed to control his anger. As he stood to his feet, Tibbs added, "The other item we need to recover will be a little easier. It's up under the bridge. And I have no doubt whatsoever that the Harper family will be pleased to hear about it."

The traffic that was piling up behind the blockage of emergency vehicles, wreckers, and a clean up crew caused a great stir of technical proportions. Cell phones, digital phones, and CB's in the hands of the curious onlookers were feeding information about the scene to those far away who would want to know about it. As Joe stood gazing at the sight, he realized he still had his camo on, and he was still holding his bow. He assumed he probably looked a little strange to those who were walking onto the scene, so he stepped to the mini-van to put his bow away and remove his face paint. As he did, he noticed that the patrol car behind the Honda still had a quiet occupant locked inside. He found Officer Tibbs and requested, "Would you do me a favor? Would you check your prisoner's pockets and see if you can find an automotive item on him? I believe he has something that might restore the *heartbeat* to my truck!"

Officer Tibbs returned within a few minutes and handed Joe the ignition coil wire that he had found in Shelby's coat pocket. "The prisoner wants you to know that he won't forget you."

Joe simply smiled. "You tell him for me, I'll not forget how he taught me to do the bullet dance this morning. And please tell him I'm deeply sorry for poking holes in him. Really, I am."

Evelyn listened to Joe's comments and stared at him with shock on her face. "Just how many times did you shoot today, Robin Hood?"

Having been referred to by that ancient name earlier in the day in a not so pleasant moment, Joe chuckled out loud. "I lost track, Evelyn. But as many times as I came to full draw in the last few hours, my arms oughta be sore tomorrow!"

As Bob unloaded the .357 that Bill had handed him, he walked over to his young neighbor. "Earl, I gotta know just one thing."

Earl knew what question was coming as he leaned on the hood of the Tanner mini-van.

Bob asked, "How is it that this fellow, Jack, knew your name? Are you involved in this craziness somehow?"

"No, sir. I had nothing to do with what happened at Harper's store last night. Jack is my former brother-in-law. He knows a part of my past that I haven't told anyone around here about."

In an effort to offer Earl the freedom to say, or not to say, more about his past, Bob responded with understanding. "Well, if you ever need anyone to jaw with about all that, I have an available ear."

Earl looked at his elderly friend in the same way a son would look at a gracious father.

Trooper Wilson joined the two men at the hood of the van. "Mr. Potter, we've gotta hurry to Giles Memorial with the ambulance, but before I go, I wanted to say thanks for your help today and... feel free to let me know if there's anything else you want to add to our files about these two guys. You'll know where to find me."

Earl paused to gather his thoughts and to drink in the unexpected blessing of the trooper not pressing him about his past. Grateful for the trust that was being shown to him, he respectfully said, "Sorry about your patrol car, Trooper Wilson. I'm glad I could be of service to you today. You'll never know how glad I am!"

As Wilson walked away, Earl realized that two of the words in the officer's statement of thanks somehow echoed in his mind— *feel free*. No sweeter words could have come to him at that moment, especially from a representative of the law. Before he could change his mind, he turned to his neighbor and said, "Bob, I escaped a fiery death today. That was a mighty close call! Since this fiasco started late last night, I've been thinking a lot about some things you and Sarah have told me more than once over the past four years. You know, things like 'getting all cleaned up inside, and ready for Heaven.'"

Bob put his hands in his pockets, looked down at the pavement, and felt the warmness in his heart that always came at the mention of Sarah's name. He shook his head in an understanding way as Earl continued. "She told me one time about another type of fire I needed to escape. Can we go to your house tonight and talk about that a little more?"

"Earl, I'd like nothing better than to end this day on a positive note. And having you at my table for a late night cup of hot coffee and some cold chicken would sure be a blessing. And...." Bob paused and thought of how much he wished Sarah could have been there to hear the young man's request, then added, "...before the day is over, I guarantee you that, from now on, you won't have to worry about any more fires."

Trooper Tibbs headed to the bridge with Shelby, who would direct him to the duffel bag. Jack was on his way to the emergency room. And with all of his friends preparing to make their way home in patrol cars and wreckers, Joe set about to gather his family. He hated to interrupt Matthew's energetic and enjoyable conversation with Stan, but he called to his son. "Let's go, Matt. You need to drive us to my pick-up!"

As Joe and Matthew climbed into their mini-van, Evelyn was ending her cell call to inform the girls of the outcome of the day. She glanced at Joe with a sympathetic look and offered her tired husband an idea that was sure to console. "Dear, the head and rack on that buck that's laying up there on the hill sure would look good over the fireplace."

Joe knew that spot in their home was reserved for items only a woman's taste would allow. Upon hearing Evelyn lovingly concede to the idea of hanging a head mount above the mantel, and knowing she was aware of the cost of taxidermy, Joe said a sincere, "Thank you, sweetheart. Thank you so much!"

As they drove away, he thought of Evelyn's gracious offer. Then another idea came to his mind. "You know, honey, I appreciate your suggestion, but if it's all right with you, there's a little market on the east end of town where I'd like to hang that deer. I have a feeling that my buck is a distant relative of the big one that's already hangin' there."